Crazy Quilt Family

Crazy Quilt Family

Vivian McDermott

ISBN: 0997055308
ISBN 13: 9780997055306
Library of Congress Control Number: 2015919309
Vivian McDermott, Shelby, MT

I

Baby Belle

February 1944
Havre, Montana

Liz's water broke late in the afternoon on the twenty-first day of February. At first, she was just uncomfortable and walking around helped, but as the contractions came closer together, they also increased in intensity. By evening, she was writhing on the bed, feeling as if her insides were being simultaneously twisted, pulled, and squeezed.

If each pain was similar to being tossed about and then flung onto the shore by the waves of a stormy sea, then Anna's voice could have been compared to a lighthouse beacon. Calm and steady, she coached Liz to surrender to the pain and let her body do its work. When Liz was able to heed her advice, the pain became slightly more bearable. When she fought against the pain it became worse. Just when Liz thought she could stand no more, the contraction eased and the pain diminished. Before she could catch up, it began again.

On and on, throughout the late night and early morning hours, with less and less time between contractions, she labored. When Anna's voice reached Liz through her haze of agony and instructed her to push, she knew she couldn't do it. In the age-old miracle of birth, her body instinctively did what was necessary, and shortly before noon, Belle made her entrance into the world, weighing just over five and a half pounds. She had all her fingers and toes, a rosebud mouth and a halo of blonde curls.

Against her better judgment, Anna had agreed to let Liz hold the baby. For what seemed like only a couple of minutes, but was in reality almost half an hour, Belle lay nestled in her mother's arms. Liz marveled at Belle's perfection and stroked her cheek, committing her features to memory.

All too soon, Anna took Belle away to deliver her into the care of her adoptive parents, and Liz turned her face into the pillow and began to sob. The pain of childbirth paled to nothing when compared to the agony of giving up her baby girl. As if from a long ways away, she heard her grandmother murmur, "Shh. You had no choice, dear. You've done the right thing. Just get some rest now."

II
Liz

Seven Months Earlier
July 20, 1943
Shelby, MT

Caroline Baxter hurried into the kitchen, snagging a dishtowel off the towel rack as she moved toward the sink where her daughter stood with her hands immersed in a sink full of hot sudsy water, staring out the window into the backyard.

"Sorry that took me so long," she said. "Edna was taking her trash out, too, and we got talking. I love having her for a neighbor. She was telling me another funny story about her cat..." Her voice trailed off as she looked from the empty drainer to the tears running down Liz's face.

"Liz? What's wrong?" she asked.

Liz shook her head, blinked, and started swishing the dishrag over the supper plates, then rinsing them and placing them in the drain rack for her mother to dry and put away. "I know you miss Drew, but you've been crying for over two weeks," Caroline persisted.

Liz's boyfriend, Drew, had left for army boot camp right after the 4th of July. Liz pressed her lips together but said nothing, tears still rolling down her cheeks.

"I'm afraid you're going to make yourself sick! You aren't eating or sleeping. I know it's hard, you have to be strong and carry on until Drew gets back." Caroline was trying to be sympathetic but seeing Liz so depressed was starting to scare her, and being scared made her irritable and impatient.

Except for the laugh lines around Caroline's eyes, the two looked more like sisters than mother and daughter, both five-feet-six, slender with blond hair and brown eyes. As soon as the dishes were finished Caroline folded the dishtowel and hung it back on the rack. In her thirty-eight years, one of the most important lessons she had learned was, life's problems needed to be faced and dealt with.

"Honey, it's time we talked about whatever is upsetting you. I'll fix us some tea." Recognizing the tone of command in her mother's voice, Liz shrugged, dried her hands and sat at the kitchen table, blotting her eyes with a tissue to stem her tears. Caroline filled the kettle, placed it on the stove, and lit the gas burner underneath it.

"Drew broke up with me," Liz said softly, a hitch in her voice. Caroline froze in the act of placing teacups onto their saucers.

"What?" she said as she turned to face Liz, one teacup still in her hand, glad to have the counter behind her for support. "I thought you were planning to get married."

"We were, but he said he might not come back, and for me not to wait for him." Liz pressed the heels of her hands over her eyes and took several deep breaths.

"Oh, dear." Caroline was at a loss for words.

Drew and Liz had been together since Liz was fifteen and each seemed to complete the other. Drew had been working with his dad on the family farm since he graduated from high school last year with plans to take over when his dad retired. Liz had graduated two months ago, and while Caroline and her husband had both hoped Liz would get a teaching certificate or secretarial training before she got married, they loved Drew, and expected Liz to marry him in the near future. Caroline continued to lean against the counter, so shocked at Liz's announcement that she nearly missed the next bombshell.

"I think I'm pregnant," Liz whispered brokenly. "What am I going to do?" She put her face in her hands and her shoulders shook with sobs. The shriek of the teakettle jolted Caroline from her stunned immobility and she busied herself making the tea and carrying the cups and the teapot to the table, her hands shaking and her mind scrambling frantically. When she had taken a seat opposite her daughter, and a couple of deep, calming breaths, she asked, "Are you sure?" Liz nodded. "How far along are you?"

"About two months," Liz whispered. "It happened on graduation weekend, and I haven't had my time of the month since the middle of May."

"Memorial Day weekend, then," Caroline said, and Liz nodded miserably. "What did Drew say?"

"He doesn't know," Liz mumbled.

"You didn't tell him?"

"I couldn't. I didn't figure it out until after he left," Liz said defensively.

"You didn't notice that your cycle didn't come in the middle of June?"

"Everything was all mixed up, Mom. Drew got his draft notice right after my graduation, so that was the first week of June. We were both upset, and he had stuff to do." She stopped and then finished in a rush. "I think he broke up with me because he finally got what he wanted." Caroline stared at her, and then shook her head.

"Boys who are just after that don't hang around for three years, Liz. Three weeks, maybe," she said firmly. "I was sure he loved you."

"It doesn't matter now, does it?" Liz burst out, betrayal and anger in her voice. "Barely a month afterwards and he broke up with me."

"When did you realize that you could be pregnant?" Caroline asked, returning to her original question.

"About a week after he left."

"I see."

"I don't know how to contact him, Mom, and I don't want to. If I told him I was pregnant, he'd be all noble and do the right thing. I'd feel like I trapped him into something he didn't want. No thanks. I'm in this by myself!" Her burst of anger seemed to drain her of energy and she slumped in her chair.

"You most certainly are not in this by yourself!" Caroline reminded her sharply. "You have a family who loves you! We'll get through it together," she persisted and then added, "But Drew has a right to know, and so do his parents."

"No! If we tell anybody, the gossip will start. You and Dad could get fired from your jobs. People will say nasty things to the boys," Liz said heatedly. "Nobody will hire me. I won't be able to go to secretarial school. I just don't know what to do!"

"You need to calm down before you make yourself sick," Caroline soothed.

"Mom, this is the end of life as we know it!" Liz said desperately.

"Let's try to find the bright side, shall we?" Caroline said, knowing she was talking to herself, too. Liz gave her an incredulous look that Caroline ignored.

"You'll be eighteen in a couple of weeks and you just graduated from high school. Think how much worse it would be if you were sixteen and had to drop out." Liz gave a reluctant nod. "And let's face it, high school graduation changes life as we knew it, anyway, right?"

"I guess," Liz shrugged.

"Have you told anyone? A friend, perhaps?" Caroline asked. Liz shook her head.

"Everyone thinks I'm upset because Drew left, so I just let them think that. I haven't told anyone he broke up with me, much less that I'm…" Liz hesitated and then went on, "And Trish is Drew's sister, so I can't tell her anything. It would put her in the middle, and I don't know if she'd be mad at me or mad at Drew." Her voice wobbled a little as she added, "I thought we were going to be sisters."

Caroline digested this and then said thoughtfully. "Well, the best way to keep something a secret is not to tell anyone. This is probably one of those times when complete honesty can end up hurting people. You'll have to tell Trish something at some point, of course. And if I were Drew's parents, I'd want to know."

"Mom! I'm not telling them. They'd want a hurry-up wedding, too. I don't want a husband who feels forced to marry me."

"I understand that, dear, but at some point, secrets always come out, so keep that in mind, and we need to do the right thing. This child belongs to Drew and his parents as much as to you and your dad and me."

"I know." Liz sighed. "But with Drew gone, his parents have enough to worry about." Caroline decided to change the subject, at least for now. She said thoughtfully, "I think, maybe in a few weeks, it would be a good idea for you to visit Grandma."

"It isn't fair to dump this on her."

"Elizabeth Jane Baxter! Your grandma loves you, and she'll want to help." Liz flushed and sat up straighter in her chair. When her mother used her full name, she knew she was pushing it.

"Sorry. I guess I'll just make things worse if I feel sorry for myself, won't I?"

"Yes, you will."

Liz took a couple of shaky breaths and wiped her eyes again. "Okay, why do you think I should go see Grandma?"

"Havre is a hundred miles from here, and nobody knows you there. Plus Grandma's neighbor and best friend is a midwife. You can go to visit your grandma without telling any lies, and you can help her with the garden and other chores and maybe look into going to school at Northern Montana College at some point. A change of scene would be a logical choice for you, given that you are through with school and your boyfriend just went off to war."

"*Ex*-boyfriend!" Liz interrupted.

Caroline ignored her comment and went on. "Staying with Grandma would give you time to think and decide what to do about things." As Caroline laid out her logic, Liz stopped crying and began to look more hopeful. When Liz went to bed, Caroline poured herself another cup of tea and sat dejectedly at the table, trying to compose a letter to her mother explaining things and asking for help.

III

Caroline & Phil

It was nearly eleven o'clock when Caroline's husband got home. At forty, Phil Baxter was lean and muscular and moved with athletic grace. He was the kind of man women admired, kids adored, and other men wanted on their team. A natural leader, he had a gift for communicating and negotiating and was often asked to be the spokesperson for co-workers or groups of citizens with a project. This particular evening he'd been speaking to the city council about putting playground equipment in one of the city's parks.

Phil was surprised to find his wife at the kitchen table in front of half a cup of cold tea, staring blankly into space, and a little worried when he noticed the letter beside her teacup. He paused by her chair to pat her shoulder and drop a kiss on her cheek.

"Thought you'd be in bed. It's late. The council meeting went longer than I expected it to, but the playground project got approved."

"I'm glad," Caroline murmured. "And I suppose you are in charge of getting it done?" She gave him a knowing look.

"I said I'd help," Phil agreed with a smile. "So, why are you still up?"

"I was talking to Liz. She just went to bed about a half hour ago."

"Did you find out what's been bothering her?" Phil asked. Caroline nodded.

"History repeats itself," she said with a sigh. "She's pregnant."

Phil folded his six-foot frame into the chair beside her and took her hand. "What are we planning to do about that? Drew should get leave after basic training, right? Before he gets his assignment, so they could get married then?"

"No wedding," Caroline replied. "They broke up."

"Broke up? No!" Phil exclaimed, frowning. He ran the fingers of his other hand through his short brown hair and turned back to her, searching her face. "Because of the baby?"

"He doesn't even know," Caroline muttered.

"Why, then?"

"He told Liz he might not come back and that she shouldn't wait for him. And she thinks he broke up with her because he got what he wanted, as she put it."

"That doesn't sound like Drew." Phil paused, fixed serious hazel eyes on her, and gave her hand a little shake. "And Caro, this is not history repeating itself."

"We planned our wedding because I got pregnant." Caroline reminded him, her eyes fixed on her teacup. Her voice dropped to a whisper. "And then I lost the baby." Phil closed his eyes for a moment. When he opened them, he spoke quietly but firmly.

"You didn't get pregnant all by yourself, Caro, and baby or no baby, I always planned to marry you. I fell for you the first time I saw you waiting tables in that little café. I waited two years for you to graduate and another year for you to go to secretarial school, remember? I loved you then, and I love you now." Caroline shifted her focus to their joined hands for a moment and then met his gaze, her brown eyes bright with unshed tears.

"I love you, too," she whispered. "This just brings it all back."

Phil gave her hand a sympathetic squeeze, glanced again at the letter and changed the subject.

"You wrote to your mother?"

"If Mom doesn't mind, I think it would be good for Liz to go see her at the end of the summer and stay until the baby comes.

"Why?"

"She and Liz have always had a special bond. Liz could keep busy helping mom and have some time to think and work things out."

"That makes sense." Phil nodded thoughtfully.

"I don't think I'd be able to be a steadying influence on Liz right now."

"I'm sure you'd do just fine. You're stronger than you give yourself credit for. But a change of scene might help and I think your mom would be good for Liz. She's a wise woman, your mother."

"She is, and her friend Anna is a midwife. Liz is worried about the gossip and how it will affect our jobs, especially mine. She's worried this will wreck our lives. She's afraid people will think she's a bad girl and we are bad parents, and that her brothers will suffer."

"People will say and think whatever they please." Phil shrugged dismissively. "I can't see that it will have much impact on Adam and John, and I really don't think the railroad cares what goes on in my life as long as I keep things running smoothly at the station. Do you think the school board would go so far as to fire you because Liz got pregnant? I don't remember a morals clause in your contract."

"No, there wasn't, and I wouldn't have signed it if there was. I've heard things about other towns not hiring married women, and putting all kinds of restrictive clauses in their contracts, but our board seems to be focused on educating our children, at least right now. Anyway, they are the ones who begged me to teach in the first place." She paused, remembering how the school board had asked her to teach typing, shorthand and basic bookkeeping. They had been very persistent. When she explained that she wasn't a certified teacher, they said they knew that, but teachers were hard to find and since she had graduated from a secretarial course and worked in an office, they thought her education and practical experience were qualification enough. She had taken the job only after making it clear that she would not tolerate any interference. The board had left her alone for the eight years she'd been teaching.

"Caro?" Phil asked, giving her hand another little shake, "Where did you go just now?"

"Oh, I was just remembering that the school board begged me to teach, and they also agreed to stay out of my hair. So no, I don't think they'll fire me, but that isn't the only issue. Liz can't support a baby on her own, and even if she lived here with us and we helped her, both of them would be the subjects of gossip. That would be a miserable life for Liz and not fair to an innocent child."

"So she will probably have to put the baby up for adoption, then," Phil said, standing up and starting to pace the length of the kitchen. His voice had taken on a deeper, slightly raspy tone and his jaw was clenched. "I'd like to get ahold of Drew and make him do the right thing!" He burst out.

"Liz said if Drew knew about the baby, he'd marry her right away, and I think she's right about that."

"Yeah, I think he would, too. But he should have known this might happen and asked some questions. He's been irresponsible."

"I'm mad at him, too. But he got drafted. He was probably worried about that as well."

"Yeah." Phil continued to pace up and down the kitchen, until he finally come to a stop in front of the table and flung his arms up in frustration. "Here I am in the same position your dad was in, and I wonder why he didn't beat me up. I want to hit something – or someone! And I don't hit people!" He shook his head and muttered, "I'm going for a walk."

Caroline watched him go out the back door. Phil didn't get upset easily, but when he did, he needed to be alone while he worked things out. She knew they would talk tomorrow, but she thought he might walk for quite awhile tonight. With a sigh she cleared the table and went down the hall to prepare for bed and then tossed and turned, unable to sleep until Phil slipped into bed just a few hours before dawn. The next morning, bleary-eyed from lack of sleep, the two of them sat at the kitchen table with cups of coffee.

"I'm frustrated because there isn't anything I can do," Phil admitted. "I wish I could fix things."

"That's how I feel too. I mean, we can try to take care of Liz. And the baby. But…"

Phil slumped in his chair as he stared glumly at his coffee. After a few moments, he sat up again and squared his shoulders. "I guess that's what we'll do," Phil said resolutely. "We'll take care of Liz and the baby and try to be the same kind of parents our parents were to us."

"Loving and supportive." she agreed with a nod.

It sounded good, Phil thought, sarcastically. It was mature and sensible, but it sure wasn't how he felt, and he wondered again how their parents had managed. This was a situation where acting like an adult was going to be a huge pain in the ass. If he could manage it at all, it would definitely be acting. He decided to walk to work, hoping that would help him get rid of some of his anger and frustration. Maybe this would be a good weekend to clean the garage, too.

IV

Mazelle & Anna

The kitchen smelled of cinnamon and fresh baked bread when Mazelle Robins arrived, which instantly lifted her spirits. She could always count on Anna to have the coffee on and something from the oven to go with it. They had been friends for years and right now she needed some advice and encouragement.

"Have you got a few minutes?" Mazelle asked.

"Sure," Anna replied cheerfully. "Coffee or tea? I just took cinnamon rolls out of the oven. I'm dieting, as usual, so I'm only going to have half, without butter, do you want the other half, or a whole one?"

"Coffee, thanks, and I'm dieting, too, so the other half without butter is perfect!" Mazelle smiled as she took a seat at the scarred wooden kitchen table. The diet remarks were a standing joke between the two of them. Neither one was really dieting, but they heard that phrase so often from most of the women they knew that they had started to toss it back and forth, too. The joke wasn't quite as funny now as it had been since butter was rationed due to the war. Both women had access to fresh whole milk from one of their neighbors and were able to make their own butter, but now it felt like a guilty luxury.

Mazelle was five-feet-eight and slender, with brown eyes and curly gray hair. She was tan and fit from all the work she did outdoors in her yard and garden.

"Did something happen?" Anna asked as she brought their coffee and cinnamon rolls to the table and sat down. Anna was younger than Mazelle by twenty years or so, also slim but not quite as tall. She had kind blue eyes in a classic oval face. Her long brown hair was turning gray. Sometimes she wore it braided and wrapped around her head, but today it fell down her back in a loose ponytail. She had laugh lines around her eyes and a sunny smile.

"I got a letter from Caro this morning." Mazelle explained Liz's situation. "Caro asked if you could deliver the baby, and I could keep her busy while she sorts things out and provide wisdom and emotional support."

"I see," Anna said. "Well, I'm glad she isn't asking too much of you!" Her remark had the intended effect of making Mazelle smile.

"Well, expectations are high when you are the wise matriarch of the family, you know!" Mazelle replied, rolling her eyes. "And Phil told me to be sure to tell you that he expects to pay your usual fee."

Anna nodded. "Of course I'll be happy to help in any way I can."

"I knew I could count on you," Mazelle said with a smile.

"How far along is she?"

"Caro said two months. Liz was pretty definite about that, so it doesn't sound like they've been intimate for very long."

"That makes things harder for Liz. She was probably feeling emotional about the new step in their relationship, and then to find herself alone and pregnant when she was expecting to be married… well, a woman's emotional state has an effect on her unborn child. I can talk to her about that," Anna mused. "Do you think we'll live to see the day when an unmarried girl doesn't have to hide her pregnancy?"

"I don't know. Society thinks it is so modern, but everyone still acts as if girls get pregnant all by themselves."

"And the babies are always innocent."

"Innocent or not, their parents are either pressured to marry or the child is given up for adoption," Mazelle agreed. "So I imagine we'll have to face that heartbreak at the end of the pregnancy." She stared off into space, her eyes sad.

"Mazelle, what is it?"

"Oh, this just brings back a lot of sad memories," Mazelle replied. Briefly, she explained about Caro's miscarriage before she and Phil were married. "Phil is a good man. Some girls aren't that lucky when they find themselves expecting a child."

"So you lost your first grandchild and now a great-grandchild might be put up for adoption. I'm sorry," Anna sympathized.

"Sometimes life is hard," Mazelle said, forcing a smile. "But we always get through it. Helping Liz is more important than dwelling on sad memories."

"Between the two of us we can get Liz through the next few months," Anna said. "And if Liz is here with you, it will give Caro and Phil a chance to work through their memories, too."

"It will be hard for everyone," Mazelle said. "But if I had to choose between a miscarriage and an adoption, I'd choose adoption every time."

"Me, too." Anna agreed and the two friends chatted over their coffee and their shared cinnamon roll for another half hour before Mazelle returned home to send a response to Caro and Liz. Then she spent the afternoon working in the garden and warmed up a bowl of homemade soup for supper. After washing the dishes, she fixed a cup of tea and picked up a pad of paper and a pen. Making herself comfortable in the rocking chair on the porch, she relaxed and sipped her tea.

She liked to sit and watch the sunset and think about things at the end of the day. Today, she thought about the next seven months til the baby was due, and as ideas occurred to her, she started making a list.

Liz would need looser fitting clothes, so they would have sewing projects to work on. Although the baby would probably have to be put up for adoption, it would be nice to make a few baby garments and possibly a quilt or an afghan to send with him or her. The garden would need to be weeded and watered, then harvested and cleaned up for winter, and there would be fruits and vegetables to preserve. Christmas would come and go quietly since Liz would not be traveling. There would be gifts to make and send to family, of course, and they would put up a tree and decorate, and probably have dinner with Anna and attend church services and programs. Holidays always encouraged her to count her blessings, and she hoped the same would be true for Liz. Winter might be a challenge, it being the last trimester of Liz's pregnancy, but they would figure things out. Maybe that would be a time for Liz to plan what she would do after the baby was born, something to keep her moving forward with the rest of her life. Or maybe she would be so pre-occupied with the idea of giving her baby up for adoption that it would be a full-time job trying to keep things positive. There was no way to tell right now. Mazelle knew it wouldn't be easy, but then some seasons of life were difficult. That's just the way life was. She sighed and set the list aside.

Her thoughts turned to the dark and lonely days after Robby had passed away, days when she was overcome with grief and loneliness and fear. It had been an effort just to get out of bed every morning and breathe in and out. She supposed Liz was feeling some of those same emotions if she was grieving the loss of her boyfriend, uncertain about being pregnant, and dreading having to give up her baby.

After Robby died, Mazelle worried about keeping the house and especially how she was going to manage financially. Thankfully, her sons, James and Pete, one in real estate and the other a lawyer, helped her lease out the farm land, which gave her enough income to live on, and she was able to keep the sturdy old farm house Robby's father had built for his bride and their family. She also leased some land to a beekeeper, and in addition to the cash rental fee, he kept her well supplied with honey. That had been especially nice with sugar being rationed. Anna kept chickens and the two of them traded eggs for honey. They had modified many of their recipes to use honey instead of sugar, so they always volunteered to bring dessert to meetings and potluck suppers. Decorative jars of honey were Mazelle's standard gifts for all occasions – she gave one to each of her friends in the various clubs she belonged to at Christmas time and handed them out for birthdays. If she had extra honey on hand, she took some to the farmer's market and the church bazaar to sell. She always included some hints on using the honey for baking, and she never brought any of those jars home.

She chuckled to herself remembering James telling her he thought she'd be fine if she just lived frugally. My goodness, she'd grown up poor and survived the Great Depression! Living frugally was a way of life for her.

The next morning Mazelle got busy cleaning Caro's old bedroom for Liz to occupy during her stay. She was glad she had re-decorated this bedroom last year. It hadn't cost very much, but at the time she had felt a little silly about going to so much trouble for an infrequently occupied guest room. She usually traveled on the train to visit her children and grandchildren instead of having them come to see her. It was less expensive for one person to travel, and she was able to be a part of whatever they were doing.

Her family was scattered all over the place and it was hard for them to get together. When Robby died, everyone came for the funeral, of course, and since then her children and grandchildren scheduled a reunion over the 4th of July, which enabled them to celebrate her birthday on the 5th.

Several of the women from her church had most of their children and grandchildren living right here in the area and sometimes Mazelle envied them their Sunday dinners and holidays with women in the kitchen, men on the porch or in the yard, little ones underfoot, and lots of conversation and laughter. She hoped one day this old house would be home to a family again and wondered if that would happen in her lifetime.

As she scrubbed, dusted and polished, Mazelle thought about Liz and wondered how this pregnancy would change her life, because she knew that it would. Years of experience had taught her that one thing leads to another until you find yourself traveling an entirely different road or living in a new place. The process in life was similar to how she had ended up redecorating this bedroom.

In Caro's day the room was painted pale yellow and there were sunny yellow gingham curtains hanging at the windows and a white chenille bedspread on the bed. Last winter, at the Penney's white sale she had looked for new sheets for that room. Funny, how a little thing like that could set your mind running.

The next month, while cleaning the basement, she found an old cotton rag rug her mom had made. It was still thick and soft, but had faded from whatever color it was originally to a non-descript mixture of off-white and gray. She looked at that rug and thought about the two boxes of dye she'd found while cleaning her cupboards, one red and one blue. Knowing that red and blue made purple, she added those two boxes of dye to a tub of hot water and threw the rug in. It turned out better than she had expected. The mixture of fabrics in the rug absorbed the dye in varying shades of purple and lavender and the new soft colors looked lovely on the wood floor beside the bed. Of course the rug did not match the yellow walls, and of course she wasn't really looking, but while in the hardware store one day not long after that, she found a gallon of lavender paint on sale. It had seemed like a sign from heaven that it was time to spruce up that room, so she bought the paint and used it on the walls, leaving the trim a pristine white. At least it was pristine after a good scrubbing.

She had known those yellow curtains wouldn't match the lavender walls, but they were over twenty years old, so she didn't feel too badly about replacing them. She looked through the material in her sewing room and found enough white cotton to make new curtains, tying them back with braided purple yarn, and she made several throw pillows from scraps of fabric in shades of lavender, pink and purple to brighten up the white chenille spread, which though old, was still serviceable. Both working on the project itself and the end result had pleased her without costing much money.

When she finished cleaning, Mazelle looked around, pleased with how nice things looked. Tomorrow she would spruce up the bathroom. Robby put that bathroom in when the boys were teenagers, remodeling the smallest bedroom, which had originally been a nursery. He did all the work himself. Goodness, that man had been so talented. He could build or repair just about anything. It was large for a bathroom, with a big claw-footed tub, two sinks on a long counter, and plenty of storage. It was rarely used now, but it would be wonderful for Liz to have a bathroom nearby, especially later in her pregnancy.

People thought this old house was too big for one old woman, but quite the opposite of rattling around the place, Mazelle enjoyed all the space. She was very comfortable here with her routine, her things and her memories.

When Robby died so unexpectedly, her children worried about her living alone and for some reason, they especially didn't want her to sleep upstairs in case she should fall down the stairs in the middle of the night. She had rolled her eyes over that, wondering if perhaps her children pictured her wandering around in the middle of the night, or maybe even sleepwalking. But, in any case, she found it difficult to sleep in their old room without Robby, and the downstairs bedroom suited her needs, so she had not protested moving there. It was a good-sized room with walls painted a soft cream color and curtains a nondescript shade of beige. She hadn't done anything more than make sure the quilt on the bed was heavy enough to keep her warm, considering it a bland room for a bland time in her life as she adjusted to living alone.

It was far from bland now, of course. Her two daughters-in-law, Sandra and Karen, had given her a bedspread and curtains in a rose print on a cream background as a Christmas gift that year. Caro had contributed a dark rose rug for the floor beside the bed and a set of flannel sheets. The new things had inspired her to do a little sprucing up of the rest of the room. She was sure Sandra, Karen and Caro had that in mind when they came up with those particular gifts.

The space between the two large windows was soon covered with family pictures in frames of all sizes. Whenever she got a new picture of her children or grandchildren, she took down the old picture and replaced it with the new one. It pleased her to see those smiling faces at the beginning and end of each day. And the rocking chair she had rocked all her babies in sat beside the window. When she sat there she could look out over the countryside toward the mountains. She didn't sit there often, but if she was having trouble sleeping, or if she was sad or sick, it was a great place for a cup of tea and some meditation time. Just looking at it and remembering that Robby had made it for her when she was pregnant that first time was a great comfort.

The old dining room was now a cozy sitting room with Robby's old roll top desk beside the door. It was where she paid her bills and kept all her paperwork. She had a comfortable armchair and a side table with a lamp for reading. They hadn't had a family sit-down dinner in years, so Pete and James had moved the dining room table and chairs to the wall between the two windows on the opposite side of the room from the desk. They were out of the way, but still accessible and near the china hutch in the corner. She enjoyed pretty things, so she topped the table with a lace tablecloth and kept her grandmother's tea set on display, often flanked by vases of fresh flowers from the garden.

The living room was quite large, spanning the entire north side of the house. It had a river rock fireplace that made winter evenings cozy and warm. The walls on each side of the fireplace were lined with bookshelves full of books, photo albums and games of all kinds. The windows between the bookshelves had roomy window seats filled with pillows, which could also be used on the floor. The children had curled up in those window seats and indulged in many a good book while growing up. Mazelle was thrilled that all three of her children had been, and still were, avid readers.

These days, her old bones were too stiff for window seats; she preferred to sit near the fireplace in a comfortable armchair with her feet propped on an ottoman to read. There was a matching armchair, a large couch and a smaller loveseat also arranged around the fireplace, each with a small table nearby. There were two other seating areas in the room: a pair of rocking chairs with a table between them at the end of the room in the corner and a loveseat and a pair of upholstered chairs on opposite sides of a coffee table along the end wall. This was the only room in the house that sometimes felt too big for one person, but it was a great place for a family gathering.

Between the housework and the yard work, Mazelle never lacked for things to do and stayed in good physical condition. She had scaled back the garden after the children left home, but still grew enough produce to share with some of her neighbors, take to the farmer's market, and preserve for her own use over the winter. The apple tree, raspberry and chokecherry bushes, and strawberry plants provided ample ingredients for jams, jellies and assorted desserts. The jams and jellies made great gifts, and of course she used them herself, too. She did her own spring and fall cleaning every year, sorting and discarding things she no longer needed so they wouldn't accumulate. Discarding was difficult, first because she tended to look at an item and think she might need it someday and second because the house had so much storage space. There was a full basement and an attic in addition to closets and cupboards. She had to make a conscious effort not to fill up all that space just because it was there.

Mazelle kept busy and stayed active, but she admitted that sometimes she was lonely. And sometimes she didn't feel like her life mattered, or at least not the way it had when she'd had a husband to share her life and children to raise. She thought she would enjoy having Liz stay with her, because, even though there was no doubt that her family loved her, feeling loved was not the same as feeling useful. Being asked to help Liz warmed her heart. It was nice to be needed again.

V

Moving On

Caroline met the mailman at the door as she had done every day this week, even on the days she knew it was too soon for a reply from her mother. Today there was a letter. She tore open the letter and scanned the contents.

> Dear Caro,
>   I would be thrilled to have Liz stay with me for the next few months, or for as long as she wants or needs to be here. Anna has assured me she will be available for moral and medical support. I spent yesterday getting your old room ready for Liz to stay in and have started a list of things that need doing in addition to the regular chores around here. Don't worry, dear, things have a way of working out if we just take the next step and do the best we can.
> Love,
> Mom

The next month flew by for Liz. She still cried herself to sleep most nights, but staying busy during the day was a welcome relief from the previous few weeks when time had seemed endless as she struggled alone with the upheaval in her life. Telling her mom had been the right thing for her to do.

"Liz!" Trish said as she sat down in the bleachers next to her friend. Petite and curvy with dark hair, Trish's blue eyes were filled with concern. "How are you doing?" Liz was watching her twelve-year-old brother John play first base. Her dad coached the Little League team and her brother Adam was his assistant.

"I'm doing okay, Trish," Liz replied, fighting to keep her voice steady. "I'm glad you're here, I wanted to talk to you." Trish raised her eyebrows and waited. "I'm going to go and visit my grandma in Havre for awhile, you know, to take my mind off things. We talked about going to school in Great Falls this fall..." her voice trailed off.

"That's okay. I'm thinking about staying home to help my dad anyway." Trish hurried to assure her.

"Thanks, Trish."

"Have you heard from Drew?"

"Not lately." She gestured to the field where John was taking his turn at bat, and after he got a hit, she managed to keep Trish busy with idle chatter about other things. She had a headache by the time she got home, but at least she hadn't burst into tears at the mention of Drew's name. Maybe that was progress, she thought.

Liz and her mother went through Liz's closet and her winter clothes, which had been packed away in a trunk, to decide what she could take with her to Grandma's house. Everything she thought she'd need fit into two medium-sized suitcases.

Usually, Liz had some of her friends for a backyard barbeque to celebrate her birthday on August 25th, and in the last several years, her birthday party had become the last summer gathering for her and her friends. This year, under the circumstances, she decided to have a quiet celebration with just the family. She asked her mother to fix fried chicken, potato salad, assorted garden vegetables and angel food cake. They all would have preferred a chocolate cake, but chocolate was impossible to get since it was used in the rations for the armed forces. Liz didn't really care what they ate, or if they ate, but she went through the motions to keep up appearances. The next week, Liz boarded the eastbound train in Shelby and within a few hours, arrived in Havre with her suitcases and a tote bag. She stepped off the train, thanked the conductor for his assistance, and moved to greet her Grandma Mazelle with a tremulous smile on her pale face.

Liz put her things in the back of the battered old pickup and climbed into the cab. Mazelle drove carefully over a bumpy dirt road to get from the train station to her house, a distance of about a mile. She hadn't gotten her driver's license until her sons learned to drive, and she still didn't drive much. Gas was rationed now, of course, but Mazelle preferred to walk anyway, sometimes she even walked into town for groceries or other supplies, pulling her garden wagon. It kept her in shape, was a pleasant physical activity, and was a lot less nerve-wracking than driving. But today, she had driven the old pickup, unsure of how much luggage Liz would have, and how she would react to an old woman pulling a wagon, or the prospect of walking home after her long train ride.

The countryside between town and farm had been consumed by homes and businesses so what had once been a farmhouse in the country, was now a big old house at the edge of town. The two-story structure was gray, either by design or because the white paint had weathered, with black shutters and a wrap-around porch. Liz caught a glimpse of the garden and the small barn that served as a garage and a storage area for yard and garden equipment, ladders and some of Grandpa's tools. He'd had a workshop in one corner of that old barn, Liz remembered. And there was a small area on this side that they called 'the bunkhouse' where the hired man used to stay during harvest.

Liz was so tired that when Grandma suggested she take a nap, she didn't protest that she didn't usually take naps. She just went to her room and slept for a couple of hours, had a light supper and went to bed early. She simply couldn't believe she was so tired, but Mazelle smiled and said part of it was the baby sapping her energy. After a few days of not doing much, Liz woke early one morning and couldn't decide if she was feeling more energetic and optimistic about the day and about life in general, or if she was just bored with sitting around doing nothing. She dressed and wandered into the kitchen while Mazelle was making toast. She had spent time here as a small child, and just as she remembered, the house was huge. This kitchen was over twice the size of her mom's. It had high ceilings and lots of cupboards and countertop, and Grandma said she used every bit of the space when she was canning or making jam or jelly, or when more than one person was cooking.

"Good morning, sweetheart!" Mazelle greeted her. "Feeling better today?"

"I guess I'm ready to do, I don't know, whatever there is to do."

"Good for you." Mazelle smiled. "I'm sure you'll be shocked to know that I made a list of possibilities." Liz surprised herself by smiling in response. She had, of course, smiled in the last month, but it had been an effort to do so, and it had been quite awhile since she had seen the humor in anything at all.

"It must be hereditary," she said. "Mom and I would both be lost without our lists."

"Think of it as good training for when you are an old lady like me and your memory needs all the help it can get!" Mazelle chuckled.

"You are not an old lady, Grandma!"

"Thank you, dear," Mazelle replied, glad to see Liz demonstrate some spirit.

"I really appreciate you letting me stay here. I'm sorry to be such a problem."

"Sweetie, you might *have* a problem, but I certainly do not consider you to *be* a problem. And you'll soon learn that life is a series of problems, one after another. Every day we get up and deal with problems, some of them big and some of them small, that's just the way it is."

"That's depressing," Liz said, trying and failing to keep the sarcasm out of her voice.

"I believe the way we deal with our problems determines what kind of people we grow into. And I think it is an honor when the people we love ask for our help with big problems, so I should probably be thanking you."

"I can't seem to stop crying," Liz muttered as she wiped tears from her cheeks. "I feel like such a disaster. I say mean things and everything makes me cry, and I can't stop thinking about…" Liz clamped her lips closed.

"Some of that is probably because you are pregnant, but you are also grieving, Liz. Crying is part of the process. So first you cry, and then you take a step forward. You might cry some more, but you keep moving forward, and eventually you will get through this."

"Okay." Liz took a deep breath and grabbed another tissue to wipe her eyes. She didn't believe a word of it, but she was a guest in her grandma's house, and her grandma was nice, so she would try to be polite, even if her life was a mess and her future was hopeless.

When they had their toast in front of them, with coffee for Mazelle and tea for Liz, Mazelle brought out the list she'd jotted down and handed it over.

"Here are some things that we could think about doing."

Liz skimmed through the list and nodded. "The first thing on the list is a visit with your friend Anna. I suppose we should do that pretty soon?"

"I think so," Mazelle responded, "Actually, Anna is coming over for dinner tonight. We eat with each other quite a bit, and I thought it would give you a chance to get to know her. Then she can do an exam and start a chart for you next week, if that's okay."

"Yeah, okay." Liz glanced at the next thing on the list. "I brought some things Mom and I thought would work for awhile, at least. But I suppose my clothes should come next." She was silent a moment, and then said hesitantly, "I'd like to make some things for the baby. I know I won't be able to keep him or her, but…" her voice trailed off and she blinked back more tears.

"That's what I thought, too," Mazelle said briskly, "Babies need clothes and blankets, and the ones made with love are the best kind. I have some old patterns in my sewing room that you can look through, both for you and for a layette. Styles haven't changed that much, so they should work, or we can adapt them. And you can also look through my material to see if there are any fabrics you like. How does that sound?"

"Sounds like a good place to start," Liz said. She was determined to have a positive attitude. Everything here was so different from what she was used to, but she had always felt comfortable with Grandma Mazelle, and that helped a lot.

When breakfast was over and they had washed the dishes, Mazelle went outside to pick the rest of the corn for freezing and Liz climbed the steps to the second floor. At the top of the stairs on the right was the lavender room she was using. It was fresh and pretty and it was comforting to know that it had once been her mother's room. Next to that was the bathroom. She knew that it had originally been a nursery, so it was a good-sized room. At the end of the hallway was her grandma and grandpa's old bedroom. It was a large room with a four-poster bed covered by a quilt in shades of brown and green. On the far wall of that room was a door that opened onto a narrow stairway leading to the attic. She had childhood memories of afternoons spent going through trunks of old clothes and playing dress-up in that attic.

On the other side of the hall were the two rooms that had once belonged to her Uncle James and Uncle Pete; one of them was decorated in shades of blue, and the other one was dedicated to sewing.

Liz spent the rest of the morning in her grandma's sewing room. The place bore no resemblance to the dining room table at home where she and her mother worked on their sewing projects. And it certainly didn't look like the boy's bedroom it had once been. The walls were pale green and all the woodwork was white.

Green-and-white-striped valances adorned the top of each window, but there were no curtains.

In one corner of the room near the window, was a triangular bench with a stool underneath it. It was odd-looking and Liz wondered what it was for. Next to that was a white L-shaped table. Grandma's sewing machine sat on one end of the table in front of a white wooden chair with a cushion covered in the same green and white stripe as the window valances. On the table was a wicker basket containing pins, pincushions, tailor's chalk, measuring tape, scissors, and other miscellaneous sewing tools. The closet door had been removed and the inside fitted with shelves from floor to ceiling, each one crammed with fabric of all colors, types, and designs. Some fabric was folded and stacked, some was in baskets and some was in boxes. On the wall between the windows was an old white dresser with two drawers full of yarn and two drawers packed with patterns. The smallest drawer on top was full of thread, an assortment of zippers, and buttons in all sizes, shapes and colors. She smiled at another memory of helping to sort buttons one rainy day when she was small. An ironing board was set up in the corner next to a three-way mirror. At first glance, Liz thought the mirror was standing on the floor, but when she looked closer, she realized that the center section was attached to the wall and the two side sections were hinged, so they could adjust for better visibility.

She realized her grandpa must have built the mirror, the table, and everything else in the room. Liz had been ten when he died, so she hadn't known him too well, but here was evidence of his craftsmanship, his love for his wife, and his support of her activities. She blinked back tears and laid her hand on her abdomen as she realized the legacy of love she would pass on to her child, even if she had to give him or her away.

Liz had come into the sewing room with full intentions of looking for material for her own clothes first, but she got sidetracked by a piece of white flannel with little yellow ducks in green raincoats and galoshes. She looked further and found both plain green and plain yellow flannel. She thought there would be enough to make a crib-sized quilt, so she laid those items on a corner of the table and turned her thoughts to her own wardrobe.

By the time Mazelle came in from the garden at lunchtime, Liz had found two pieces of corduroy, one in burgundy and one in chocolate brown, and some navy blue denim that would make warm jumpers and look nice with blouses and sweaters that she had brought with her.

Liz helped Mazelle freeze corn that afternoon and then they worked together on supper preparations.

"Come on in!" Mazelle called in response to a knock on the door, and a moment later, Anna appeared in the kitchen, smiling.

"Something smells good!"

"Vegetable soup and cornbread," Mazelle said. "And just so you know, I fully intend to ignore my diet and slather my cornbread with butter and honey. I just made a batch of fresh butter!"

Anna laughed and said, "Me, too." Liz was giving them quizzical looks, so after the introductions, Mazelle explained the dieting joke she and Anna shared. Liz thought that was a little corny, but Anna was easy to talk to and before long they were seated at the table chatting amiably over their supper.

One morning the following week, Mazelle and Liz walked to Anna's house. Anna was Mazelle's nearest neighbor, though that didn't mean she lived next door. It was about a tenth of a mile down Mazelle's driveway, across the road, another tenth of a mile or so to the right, and then a left turn into Anna's driveway, which was about half as long as Mazelle's.

Anna's house was a sprawling stone cottage with a chimney on one end, nestled in amongst an assortment of trees. There were several cottonwoods, a handful of pine and fir trees, and a couple that looked like aspen. Not that Liz knew a lot about trees. There was a garden off to one side, an apple tree in the front yard and flowers tumbling from assorted baskets and pots lining the path to the back door.

Sunlight poured through the window over the sink in Anna's kitchen, bathing the small pots of herbs on the windowsill in golden light. The cupboards were a honey-colored pine and the walls were a creamy white. The round wooden table was covered in a red-and-white-checked tablecloth and the wooden chairs had matching checked cushions. There were red towels and potholders on display, and the pottery mugs Anna was filling with coffee for herself and Mazelle and tea for Liz were red as well. Liz noticed a painting beside the door that appeared to be fairies dancing under a rainbow.

"This is a bright, cheerful room, Anna," Liz said politely. Anna smiled her acknowledgement of the compliment.

"I'll leave you two to get down to business," Mazelle said as she took her cup of coffee outside and sat on the porch in a rocking chair while Anna talked to Liz in the kitchen. On the way home, Mazelle asked how the checkup had gone.

"Mostly paperwork, height and weight and approximate due date," Liz replied. "Anna said that women have been having babies for all of history and that our bodies know what to do. So I just have to be sensible about eating, sleeping, and getting exercise."

"A lot of life is just plain old common sense," Mazelle agreed.

"And I'm supposed to try to be happy, or at least calm and content," Liz said sarcastically.

"Do you think you can do that?" Mazelle asked. "Be happy?"

"What do I have to be happy about, exactly?" Liz asked.

Mazelle did not reply until they got home. "Time usually helps," she said mildly as they stepped onto her porch. "And a good attitude helps too."

Liz tried to keep her inner turmoil under control, at least during the day, by keeping busy. She felt terrible whenever she snapped at her grandmother, but sometimes the words slipped out before she could stop them. The hours she spent alone in her room in the middle of the night were hard, too. She either tossed and turned or dreamed about Drew. Most mornings she woke up with a wet pillow and eyes red and puffy from her tears.

As September gave way to October, Liz and her grandma fell into a rhythm of working in the kitchen in the morning after breakfast, canning or freezing garden produce or making a batch of jam or jelly. Liz grew up helping her mother do these same fall chores so she knew her way around the kitchen, and she and her grandma worked well together.

Afternoons were spent in the sewing room. Within a few weeks, Liz had four loose fitting blouses and three jumpers to wear over them. They had finished the soft flannel quilt and turned their efforts toward sewing a layette for the baby. It was obvious that this was not the first time Grandma had sewn things for babies and expectant mothers, judging from the patterns and fabrics she had in her sewing room. They made a dozen tiny gowns and little shirts and twice that many diapers, all soft flannel and cotton mostly yellow and green, some pale blue, and white. Grandma even had two sets of diaper pins to include.

Liz found it both odd and comforting that she hadn't gone out much since she had come to her grandma's house. It was odd because at home, she would have been a lot more social, and it was comforting to be able to focus on sorting things out in her mind and getting ready for the baby without the distraction of worrying about what people were saying or thinking. Nobody here seemed to care about the more personal details of her life, or if they did, they refrained from asking questions. She didn't know if that would change once she started to show.

Mazelle continued to go about her routine, taking produce to the farmer's market every Wednesday, not seeming to mind when Liz preferred to stay at home. She had a weekly Bible study group and belonged to a garden club and a book club. Each of those met every other week in someone's home, so she had something scheduled every week of the month. Last week it had been Mazelle's turn to host the book club, and Liz helped make huckleberry shortcake, and had set up a buffet on the dining room table with fall placemats, the tea things, and the china dessert plates. She'd refused to linger downstairs to meet the ladies and socialize a little before the meeting, preferring to stay in her room. The Bible study group was coming next week and Mazelle planned to serve vegetable soup and homemade breadsticks for lunch, but hadn't decided about dessert yet.

Mazelle and Anna attended church together most Sundays, and after the first two weeks Liz had been going with them, even though she would rather have stayed at home. She'd gone to church regularly her whole life, and she liked that part of her weekly routine, but now she was so mixed up and moody that she didn't want to smile and be nice to people. Her grandma had said it would be good for her, and so she went. It took a few weeks to get used to the fact that one Sunday they attended Anna's church and the next week they went to Mazelle's. Anna was Lutheran and Mazelle was Methodist, and Liz noticed that the services were quite similar. Once she got used to switching back and forth, she enjoyed the two different congregations.

"How did you and Anna decide to go to each other's churches?" Liz asked one Sunday as they were enjoying a bowl of soup after church.

"Oh, we both walk to church and we used to visit on the way and then go to our separate services," Mazelle replied. "One day we were so busy visiting that I missed my turn, so I just went in with Anna."

"The next week, I made the turn with her and went to the Methodist church," Anna remembered. "And after that we just started alternating."

"It wasn't something I thought much about and made a decision to do, although I do try to arrange my life so I don't get too set in my ways," Mazelle said with a laugh.

"Me, too," Anna agreed. "Routines are good, as long as there is a reason for them, but so often people get in a rut and become narrow-minded. We don't want to do that!"

"No, we don't!" Mazelle exclaimed.

Liz found the interaction between the two women amusing and informative. They seemed to really think about things and have a reason for the things they did.

In the evenings, Liz and Mazelle listened to the news and other radio programs, read, played cards or checkers, or wrote letters. Liz enjoyed those evenings, but she dreaded the nights that followed when she was either unable to sleep or having bad dreams about Drew.

VI

Trish

Trish turned off the highway onto their farm road and stopped the pickup. She walked to the rural mailbox set on a post embedded in the ground beside the road and retrieved the pile of mail inside. Sorting through it as she walked back to the pickup, she found a letter addressed to her and left it on top of the pile that she placed on the seat beside her. Liz had never written her a letter before, and she was afraid this one would not be good news, so she decided to wait until she was in her room to read it.

> Dear Trish,
>
> I should have told you this in person, but I just couldn't do it. Drew broke up with me right before he left. I'm going to stay with my grandmother and try to figure out what to do next. I can't put that part of my life behind me and go on and still be your friend, because there are just too many memories of Drew mixed up in my friendship with you. I know this will hurt you. It hurts me as well. I'm very, very sorry.
> Liz

Trish sat there for a long time before she stood and made her way to the kitchen to help with supper. Jean Edwards looked up from her place by the stove. She was petite and curvy like her daughter, with the same blue eyes and dark hair.

"There you are! Could you set the table please, dear?"

"Sure, Mom," Trish replied, and as she arranged plates, silverware and glassware, she told her mother about the letter from Liz.

"Drew broke up with her?" her mother exclaimed in disbelief. "Why on earth would he do that? He told us he planned to marry that girl!"

Trish shrugged miserably. "Oh Trish, honey, I'm sorry." Jean patted Trish's shoulder in sympathy. "I guess I can understand Liz wanting a clean break with you and everything connected with Drew. But it's sad for both of you girls. You were as close as sisters." Jean shook her head in bewilderment. "I can't figure out why he would break up with her in the first place. It doesn't make sense."

"Drew got real quiet and looked like he wasn't sleeping very well that week or so before he left, remember?" Trish said. "The other guys who got drafted were kind of, oh, like they get before a football game, you know, acting all tough and brave. And they really hammed it up at the 4th of July parade."

"I remember," Jean agreed, "Drew didn't even go to the parade, much less ride in it."

Trish and her mother continued to discuss the topic throughout their evening meal. Jean's husband listened closely to their conversation but didn't say much. John never really said very much. He was a quiet man, the kind a woman could depend on. He was tall with broad shoulders, serious gray eyes and dark hair going white at the temples. Jean had loved him since they were in high school together, years before he even knew she existed.

"Mom?" Trish asked, as she helped with the dishes. "Dad went to war, didn't he?"

"He did, yes," Jean replied.

"Did that cause problems between you?"

"No," Jean said. "We weren't seeing each other then."

"You weren't?" Trish asked in surprise. "I thought you went to high school together."

"We were in high school at the same time, but I was two years younger, and, well… he had a girlfriend then," Jean explained.

"Who was it?" Trish demanded. "Do I know her? What did she look like?"

"You ask so many questions, Trish! Her name was Tammy, she was tall and blonde with brown eyes, and she seemed nice enough. I didn't know her, really. She got married and moved away years ago," Jean said without going into detail about how John and Tammy were the most popular couple in school, how they had seemed perfect for each other, and how everyone had expected them to get married soon after graduation. Then, just like now, the war intervened in their lives and John went off to fight. Jean had, of course, heard the gossip about Tammy running around while John was overseas. It was hard to avoid hearing things like that in a small town. Then suddenly, Tammy got married and moved away and there were rumors about that as well. There were always rumors and gossip, much as Jean wished there weren't.

"So if you two didn't date in high school, how did you get together then?" Trish persisted, bringing Jean out of her reverie.

"Grandpa Joe broke his leg and had to be in the hospital for a couple of weeks," Jean explained. "I had just started as a nurse's aide and he was one of my patients, so your dad and I ran into each other when he came to visit." She had assumed her schoolgirl crush on John was a thing of the past, but just being in the same room with him made her nervous and tongue-tied.

"So Dad asked you out then?" Trish prompted. "And then you got married."

"Yes, he asked me out, and the next year we got married." She had been surprised when right before Joe was to be released from the hospital, John asked her to have coffee with him. She assumed he had concerns about his dad, perhaps questions about his home care, so she had agreed. But when they were seated in a booth in the café on Main Street, he'd looked at her with those serious gray eyes.

"With Dad coming home, I won't be seeing you at the hospital anymore," he said. She hadn't known how to respond, so she just sat there, watching the spoon go around and around as she stirred her coffee. "But I would like to keep seeing you."

"You would?" She had looked up in surprise.

"Yes, very much," John replied as one corner of his mouth quirked up into a smile. "Would you come to the dance with me on Friday night?" She had stared at him until he repeated the question, and then said she would, her face beet red with embarrassment. She wondered what he saw in a girl who could barely string two words together in his presence. She agonized over what to wear and had trouble keeping her mind on the conversation at the dance, too, but John had asked her out again after that. Eventually, she relaxed around him, and they dated for nearly a year before he asked her to marry him.

They'd been seeing each other for about six months when she got up the nerve to ask him about Tammy, and he said, "She didn't turn out to be the kind of woman I thought she was. I'm glad I found that out. And glad I found you."

"Mom?" Trish said, and Jean realized that it was the second or third time she'd said it.

"Hmm?"

"Do you think there's hope that Drew and Liz will work this out and get back together?"

"I don't know, dear," Jean replied. "But I like to think there is always hope."

VII

Hearts & Minds

"Oh!" Liz exclaimed one evening, looking up from her book and quickly placing her hand on her abdomen.

"Did you feel the baby move?" Mazelle asked.

"I think so. I felt something, anyway. Anna told me I would one of these days. It feels – funny. Good funny, but not like anything else I've ever felt. I can see why Anna said it was hard to describe."

"That first kick was always when I really felt connected to my babies," Mazelle reminisced.

"I thought I would be able to keep my distance, you know, because I can't keep this baby," Liz said sadly. "But that isn't going to work, is it?"

"No, I don't think so. We're in October, dear, and you've had this baby growing in you for months now," Mazelle replied sympathetically. "Anna and I think that babies know whether or not they are loved, even before they're born. So loving your baby – even when you know it will break your heart not to keep him or her – is the best choice. Does that make sense?"

"Yes," Liz whispered. "Anna talked to me about that, too. But it's hard. It will be even worse than when Drew broke up with me, won't it?"

"A mother's love is different than the love between a man and a woman. But to answer your question, yes, I think it will be worse." Mazelle was quiet for a couple of moments. "I'm sorry, Liz. I wish it could be different. Sometimes life breaks our hearts, and we just have to get through it."

"One day at a time," Liz said with a watery smile. "Right?" Mazelle nodded.

It was easier said than done, Liz thought as she tossed and turned in her bed later that night. Every day Liz tried to stop thinking about Drew and get on with her life, but she didn't seem to be doing a very good job of it. She still thought about him during the day, despite her best efforts. And she dreamed about him at night, or perhaps it was more accurate to say that she had a recurring nightmare about the night he broke up with her.

The nightmare began with her waiting for Drew to pick her up for their date on Friday night. She'd been sad because it was the last time she would see him except for the parade the next day. There were eight other young men also scheduled to leave for basic training Saturday afternoon, and the townspeople had decided to have them lead the 4th of July parade that morning, as a way of showing them the community was proud of their patriotism and would be thinking about them and praying for them. They were to ride at the head of the parade on a flatbed truck decorated with American flags, and red, white and blue crepe paper. The high school band would march behind their float, and it was a good thing Main Street was only three blocks long, because the band knew just three patriotic songs: "The Star Spangled Banner," which they played before every ball game, "God Bless America" and "Yankee Doodle." Drew seemed preoccupied when he came to the door, his gray eyes serious and his mouth set in a grim line. He didn't tell her she looked nice, the way he usually did, or call her "Lizzie, my love." She thought they were going to a movie, but he drove silently out to the picnic area by the river and parked the pickup. Liz's heart started to pound and her mouth got dry. Something was very wrong.

"We need to talk," Drew said, finally, without looking at her. Liz twisted her fingers together in her lap. This did not sound like the proposal she had been hoping for and half expecting. Before she could respond, Drew turned to her and said in a rush.

"I don't want you to wait for me."

"What?" she said in shock. "Why not?"

"I don't know how long I'll be gone, or even if I'll come back," Drew replied, his voice was flat and he had shifted his gaze away from her. "It isn't fair for your life to be in limbo."

"You're breaking up with me?" Liz asked in dazed disbelief.

"I don't want to, but I think it's the right thing to do," Drew said expressionlessly.

"But, Drew, I've loved you since I was fifteen years old. I *want* to wait for you."

"You should get on with your life," Drew said stubbornly.

"But we've been talking about getting married, and having a family, and living on the farm. Was all of that a lie, then?"

"No!" Drew burst out, then clenched his jaw and closed his eyes. "War changes everything."

Liz sat rigid, arms clasped around her middle as if to hold herself together as tears slipped down her cheeks. One thought screamed through her mind. Drew didn't love her anymore! He wasn't just leaving her to go off to war, he was leaving her - forever.

"I want to go home," she whispered.

Drew sat completely still, his hands clenching and unclenching on the steering wheel. Twice he seemed about to say something, but stopped, and finally he started the pickup and drove back to town in silence.

Liz already had her hand on the door handle when Drew pulled to the side of the street in front of her house. She flung the door open and ran. Bursting through the door, she stumbled blindly to the bathroom and was violently sick. When there was nothing left in her stomach, she rinsed her mouth and dragged herself to her room, moving as if she were slogging through wet cement. Still fully clothed, she crawled into bed and cried herself to sleep. Night after night, the nightmare came, and she woke up with swollen eyes and tears on her pillow.

Liz had no way of knowing that Drew also had a recurring nightmare. He went to sleep thinking about Lizzie every night. It was one way to combat the reality of war, of course, but Drew loved Lizzie with all his heart. She was part of his very being.

His dream always began with the day he found the rings. He'd been looking for months, using his spare time to check every jewelry store in the area. Not quite sure what he was looking for, he recognized it immediately when he found it. The band of the engagement ring was in the form of a sideways figure eight with a modest diamond nestled in the middle, and that same sideways figure eight was etched into the gold of the wedding band. The jeweler said it was the sign for infinity. The symbol expressed the conviction in his heart. He could barely contain his happiness. He was waiting for Liz to graduate and then he planned to propose amid flowers and candlelight. He had already made the reservations at a nice place in Great Falls for the middle of June. At that point, the dream took a nasty turn and became a kaleidoscope of fear, heartache, and regret. The images swirled and he couldn't stop them: his draft notice,

Lizzie crying, him shooting at other men, Lizzie running away from him, a jeep blowing up in front of him, his fist stuffing the little black velvet box into the back of his sock drawer, his parents crying, his own flag draped coffin, Lizzie with someone else. Sometimes the images repeated in a loop he couldn't escape until daybreak. Other times the nightmare woke him and he spent the hours before dawn deathly afraid that he had lost Lizzie forever.

VIII

Choices

It was a quiet November evening at home, and Liz was reading as Mazelle sat at her desk writing a letter. The time was coming soon for Liz to make a decision about her baby.

"Grandma?" Mazelle looked up. "When I saw Anna today, she asked me if I've decided about adoption."

"I suppose it is time to think about that, yes." Mazelle sighed and put her pen down.

"Anna told me about the Florence Crittenton home in Helena and gave me this pamphlet to read. It's quite interesting. Did you know that there are Crittenton homes all over the United States? And that their mission is to rehabilitate wayward girls and fallen women?"

"I know unmarried girls sometimes go there to have their babies," Mazelle replied. "That place has been around for years."

"They came to Helena in 1896." Liz read from the pamphlet then looked up and said sarcastically. "I wonder if I'm a wayward girl or a fallen woman. Does the difference have to do with age, or the number of pregnancies you have without being married?" Mazelle sat quietly, her steady gaze resting on Liz.

"Well?" Liz said. "My whole life is ruined!"

"Your whole life will be what *you* make of it. Everyone has tough things to deal with."

"I feel like Dorothy in *The Wizard of Oz*, you know, when she said she guessed she wasn't in Kansas anymore. I was going to get married and live on the farm. Then suddenly I find myself on a yellow brick road going somewhere else, expecting a baby with no marriage in sight." Liz stared moodily at the pamphlet, blinking rapidly. When she had composed herself again, she went on.

"Anyway, according to this, it's just been in the last ten years or so that girls have been encouraged to give their babies up for adoption. Before that, most of the girls kept their babies, and a lot of them just stayed at the home."

"Did Anna recommend that you have the baby there?" Mazelle asked curiously.

"Anna doesn't really recommend anything specifically. She just gives me information and lets me make my own decisions. I really like that about her," Liz replied.

"Are you considering having the baby in Helena?" Mazelle wanted to know.

"I don't think so," Liz said slowly. "Anna told me that she often hears from people interested in private adoptions. Right now she knows of two couples who aren't able to have children of their own, so a private adoption could be arranged, if I want to do that. It's a lot to think about."

"Yes, it is," Mazelle agreed.

"Maybe it would make me feel a little better if my baby had parents who couldn't have their own baby," Liz commented. "Maybe. Oh, I don't know! I guess I need to think about it some more."

By the beginning of December, Liz and Mazelle were finishing up their Christmas gifts for members of their family. Usually, Mazelle spent Christmas with one of her three children, but because of the war, nobody thought it odd that she was spending the holiday at home. None of them except for Liz's parents knew about the pregnancy, and they all thought Liz had come to stay with her to keep her company and help with the fall chores around the house and garden. Mazelle let them think what they pleased, as it suited her purpose, and protected Liz and her unborn child. Of course they would be told what was really going on, eventually, but Mazelle thought the decisions about that should be made by Liz and her parents, and she was planning to stay out of it.

Liz made knitted hats and mittens for her brothers and her dad and a scarf and mittens for her mother. Mazelle had been working on family photo albums for her three children and their families. She and Liz would also send a package of jams, jellies and homemade candy to each family, and also give one to Anna. They planned to have Christmas dinner with Anna, too. She was away from her family for the holidays; at least Liz thought she must be. She didn't really know much about Anna or her family.

One evening as they sat in front of the fire, Mazelle noticed that the knitting needles had been quiet for a good ten minutes and Liz seemed lost in thought, gazing into the fire.

"Are you alright, Liz?" Mazelle asked.

Liz looked up, her eyes sad. "I was just thinking. Do you know that my dad is the only one in our family who can tie a decent bow?"

"Why did that little tidbit come to mind?" Mazelle asked curiously.

Liz looked into the fire again and seemed to be choosing her words carefully. "I've been going round and round about keeping the baby or doing a private adoption. One day I think I could manage on my own, maybe stay here with you and tell people I'm a widow or something. But that would be a lie, and I'd have to tell other lies to keep it covered up." Mazelle nodded, but did not speak.

"Then I think I could just not care what people say or think and raise my baby without being married. It's been done before by the girls and women who went to the Crittenton Home. But then I wonder what kind of life my child would have. She would be fighting gossip and prejudice every day." Mazelle nodded again.

"Have you decided that the baby is a girl then?"

"I've always thought so, and it's easier than saying *he* or *she* or *it*. I hate referring to my baby as *it*!" Liz replied, her voice thick.

"I do, too," Mazelle agreed.

"So just now I was remembering all the things my dad did for me. He's the one who tied bows on my dresses and for my hair. Mom's were always crooked." Liz blinked back tears. "And he taught me to ride a bike and helped me with my algebra and listened to my book reports."

"He's a good man," Mazelle agreed.

"So I guess I've finally decided that the best chance my baby has is to have two parents who love her. Moms and dads each have something different to offer." Liz swallowed hard and wiped her eyes. "I'm going to tell Anna tomorrow that I want to do a private adoption."

"Sometimes we have to make difficult choices, dear," Mazelle said, her heart aching for her granddaughter. "I'm proud of you for all the thought and love you put into making this one. And for what it's worth, I think you are making the right decision for your baby."

It was the week after New Year's when Mazelle heard a knock on the kitchen door one morning just as she took a pan of huckleberry muffins out of the oven.

"Anna! You're out early today!" Mazelle exclaimed, holding the door open. "Come in out of the cold. I have muffins."

"They smell wonderful!" Anna said as she toed off her boots and pulled off her coat, scarf, and mittens. "I wanted to talk to you about something, hopefully before Liz is up."

"She's been sleeping a little later, so we probably have a half hour or so."

"I'll get right to it then, and I can give Liz an exam after she has breakfast if she wants me to, so she won't have to go out in the cold." The two women settled at the kitchen table with coffee and muffins, and Anna got right to it.

"I need some advice."

"Okay. And you already know that my advice has no guarantee of being *good* advice." Mazelle said with a smile. Anna returned her smile and began to explain.

"Liz wants to put her baby up for adoption," Anna said.

Mazelle sighed. "This hasn't been an easy decision for her or the family."

"She says she trusts my judgment but wants to have some say on who the parents are."

"That makes sense," Mazelle agreed.

"I have been approached by two young couples in the past six months who are unable to have children. Both of them are in their late twenties, and from what I can see, they are good citizens, go to church, have good marriages."

"But?" Mazelle prompted when Anna fell silent.

"But last week I got a letter from my nephew, my brother's son. His wife had her fourth miscarriage last year, and her doctor doesn't think she will be able to conceive again, much less carry a child to term."

"How awful for them," Mazelle murmured. "So did he ask you if you could help them adopt a child?"

"Not directly, no. He asked if I had any connection to the Florence Crittenton Home and if I could give him some advice on how to go about adopting a child."

"I'm not sure what the problem is, exactly," Mazelle said.

"I think my nephew and his wife would be excellent parents – I know about their ancestors, you see." A fleeting smile appeared on Anna's face before she sobered and went on. "And on the other hand, I'm not sure if it would be ethical for me to present them as a possibility to Liz."

"I see." Mazelle nodded. She thought for a moment, and then added, "If you were planning to present the other two couples as possibilities, couldn't you present all three couples to Liz and let her decide? All of the information is general, right?" Anna nodded. "Liz wouldn't know that one of the couples was related to you. If she chooses one of the others, then so be it. If she chooses your nephew, well, it is her child's future that is being decided. I think she should have as much information and as many choices as possible."

"That's what I thought. I'm glad we agree." Anna smiled in relief just as Liz came into the kitchen, dressed in a pale yellow blouse under a chocolate brown corduroy jumper.

"Mmmm, you made muffins!" Liz exclaimed. "Hi Anna, it's always nice to see you, but it's especially nice on cold snowy days when I have a checkup. Now I won't have to go outside."

The three women chatted amiably over muffins and coffee and then Anna gave Liz a quick checkup and said she and the baby were both doing fine.

"Grandma," Liz said, when Anna had gone. "Is Anna okay?"

"She's fine as far as I know, dear. Why?"

"She looked a little pale, like she hadn't slept well or something," Liz said. "What's her story, anyway?"

"Her story?" Mazelle repeated.

"Yeah, I know she's younger than you are. I wondered if she was widowed, if she has children, and how she got to be a midwife. Now that I think of it, I don't even know her last name."

"This is the first time you've been curious about Anna," Mazelle commented.

"Well," Liz said slowly, looking down at the table. "My life is such a mess I haven't cared about much of anything else, you know?" Mazelle nodded. "Sometimes it helps to keep busy and think about other stuff." She shrugged. "So I need something else to think about, besides Drew and giving my baby away. Can you tell me about Anna?"

"I can." Mazelle smiled in sympathy. "Let's have some tea while I fill you in, shall we?"

"Good idea and maybe another huckleberry muffin. I think the baby is still hungry." Liz forced a smile. Once they were settled at the table with tea and a muffin for Liz, Mazelle began.

"I've known Anna for about fifteen years, and you are right; she is younger than I am, and older than your mother. I'm not sure exactly, and I've never asked, but I think she's about forty-five or forty-six. Her last name is Winslow, and I met her shortly after she moved in next door when I took over some mail that got delivered here by mistake. I commented that in addition to being neighbors, we shared a name."

"Um, what name? Liz frowned in puzzlement.

"Her name is actually Annabelle, and my middle name is Maybelle, so we have the Belle part in common," Mazelle explained.

"Oh, okay." Liz nodded, and Mazelle continued.

"It was a good conversation starter. She laughed and said she preferred to be called Anna, and then invited me in for coffee and we had a nice chat. Later I learned that her family lived in Wyoming and that's where she was born and raised. Her dad was a doctor and her mom was his nurse. The whole family seems to have gone into medicine, her older brother was a doctor and her older sister became a nurse."

"So how did she end up in Montana?" Liz asked.

"I'm getting to that." Mazelle sipped her coffee. "Anna was about twelve when her mom died in an accident of some kind. Her older brother and sister were grown up and gone by then so it was just Anna and her dad."

"Oh. That's sad!" Liz exclaimed.

"Yes," Mazelle agreed. "Anna started helping her dad with his patients, just like her mother had done, and her dad taught her a lot about medicine. He also mentored several aspiring doctors over the years, and Anna fell in love with one of them when she was in high school. They got married right after she graduated. He was in medical school while she went through nurse's training. They studied together, so she learned a lot of things from his lessons and they planned for her to be part of his practice. Then our country got involved in World War I, he went off to war, and was killed."

"Poor Anna!" Liz exclaimed.

"Anna said there were too many memories and she needed to start over somewhere fresh. She came here and worked for Dr. Greyson for about fifteen years. He discovered that pregnant women were more comfortable with Anna than they were with him, so he gradually let her handle most of their care until the actual delivery. And sometimes he wasn't available for the delivery, so Anna did that, too."

"And that's how she got to be a midwife?"

"That's my understanding. In rural areas like this, doctors are spread pretty thin, so nurses pick up the slack. I think she also got more training during the time she worked with Dr. Greyson, but I'm not clear about that."

"And she never fell in love again?" Liz asked.

"Apparently not. I imagine at first she was too sad, or maybe she got involved in her work and was too busy. She's never said much about that and I didn't ask."

"You said she worked for fifteen years, and then what happened?" Liz wanted to know.

"Well Dr. Greyson retired and the new doctor who took his place didn't want her to work for him. Which was not very smart, in my opinion, but he was young and full of himself," Mazelle replied.

"Isn't that funny? You'd think that the older doctor would be the one with the old-fashioned ideas about medicine being for men only," Liz mused.

"And it turned out to be the younger doctor who thought that she couldn't be of any value. It's hard to say why he decided that, but by then she had established a good reputation in the community, so she decided to see how things went."

"And things have gone well for her?" Liz asked.

"The first thing that went well was that Dr. Greyson asked her if she wanted to buy his place. She did, and that's when she moved in next door. People were already used to coming there for help, because Dr. Greyson had his office in his home. So people started to call on her for different medical issues. If she could help them, she did, and if she couldn't she sent them to a doctor or to the hospital. She stays busy, but has enough time to garden and do some painting. She's made a nice life for herself here."

"She paints?" Liz asked in surprise.

"Yes. That watercolor by the fireplace in my living room is one of hers."

"The one of the sun setting over a pond?" Liz asked. Mazelle nodded.

"She gave it to me for Christmas last year. And there is one in her kitchen that you may have noticed."

"Fairies dancing under a rainbow. I love that picture!"

"I do, too. It's one of her more whimsical ones," Mazelle agreed. "I think she's pretty good. I'm trying to get her to take them to the church bazaar to sell, but she hasn't done it."

"She has made my life so much easier that it could have been, but doesn't she miss her family?" Liz asked. "Are they still in Wyoming? Does she ever get to see them?"

"Before the war she traveled to Wyoming a couple of times a year, and I imagine she will again when things get back to normal. Right now, they stay in touch with letters, just like our family does," Mazelle replied.

Liz sat for a long time and then she said soberly, "I'll have to start over, too, like Anna did after her husband died, won't I? After the baby comes, I mean."

"I think so, yes," Mazelle replied.

"I should start thinking about that, then," Liz said thoughtfully as she picked up her empty teacup and took it to the sink. Liz had only ever seen herself marrying Drew and having a family. Now she started to consider a lifestyle like Anna's, without a family, but with a career. It was something new to think about, and she really, really needed something new to think about.

IX

Prospective Parents

In mid-January, Anna gave Liz an envelope containing general information on three young couples interested in adopting a baby. Liz read and re-read the sparse information on each of the three couples and pondered what to do. Should she do the choosing, or leave it up to Anna?

"Grandma?" Liz asked one evening later that week as they sat in front of the fire, each with a book. Mazelle looked up.

"I didn't think you were reading, Liz, you haven't turned a page in over ten minutes. What is it?"

"Anna gave me information on three couples who want to adopt a baby. It's really general – ages and occupations and not much else," Liz explained. "She said if I want to pick one, she'll go with my choice, and if I don't want to, she'll choose for me, and she will handle all the details. By the way, are my parents paying her?"

"Yes. Your dad insisted on paying her usual fee, so that's all taken care of," Mazelle replied. "So do you have a feeling one way or the other about any of the three couples?"

"Well, one couple lives on a farm and has lots of extended family around, including both sets of parents. That would be a good environment for a baby, don't you think?"

"It sounds wholesome and loving, yes," Mazelle replied.

"And one of the men is a pastor of a small church and his wife helps with his ministry. They would probably make good parents, too," Liz continued.

"You would think so. They must be caring to be in the ministry."

"The other couple has been married the longest, eight years. He works in a hospital. But get this: they've had four miscarriages. Four! How heartbreaking. So sad to think of losing one baby, but four..." Liz shook her head in sympathy.

"I can't imagine," Mazelle said.

"Neither can I." Liz was quiet for a few minutes and then asked, "Did you have any miscarriages?"

"I lost a baby between Pete and your mother. I cried for weeks," Mazelle said soberly. "Sometimes I still wonder what that child would have been like." Both of them were silent for a few minutes and then Mazelle asked, "So do you feel sorry for them?"

"Of course I do, I think anybody would," Liz replied. "Mostly I admire them because they didn't give up, even after all that heartache. That's amazing, don't you think?"

"Yes, I think they must have a lot of strength and courage," Mazelle agreed.

"I'm going to think on it for a couple more days and then talk to Anna," Liz concluded. A few more days did not change Liz's mind, and she told Anna which couple she preferred so she could start making the adoption arrangements.

The next week, Liz spent every evening in her room after supper. Mazelle let her be, assuming that she was more tired than usual. One morning, Liz came downstairs with a piece of paper in her hand.

"Could you read this and tell me what you think?" she asked. Mazelle took the paper and read:

Hello, I believe my child is a girl, and in my heart I have named her after the two women who have kept me sane through my pregnancy. My grandma's middle name is Maybelle, and her friend Annabelle is my midwife. I honor both of these women by referring to my baby as Belle. I fully expect you to choose a different name for her (or him, if I'm wrong and the baby is a boy) but giving my baby a name makes me feel better.

All I know about you is how old you are, what you do for a living and that you have not been able to have children of your own. Yet, somehow, I believe you will be good parents or I would be unable to entrust you with my child.

I am convinced that at some point in her life, Belle will ask about me and want to know why I gave her up. When she does, please tell her that I loved her very much. Explain that I wanted the best for her and knew that I could not provide it.

I give you my word that I will never try to contact you or her, but if she ever wants to contact me, I would welcome the opportunity to see her again, to talk to her and to answer her questions.

It will break my heart to give her up, but it must be done. I leave her in your care.

Sincerely,

Elizabeth Jane Baxter

Mazelle finished reading, wiped her eyes with a tissue and cleared her throat. "It's a beautiful letter, and I thank you for naming her after Anna and me, even if it's only in your heart. Somehow, I've always thought of her as a girl, too." She paused and then asked, "Why did you sign your name?"

"It's just that I've been trying to put myself in her place. Belle's I mean, to imagine how she'll feel when she understands that her own mother gave her away." Liz paused to blink back tears and steady her voice, and then blurted out. "She's going to have all kinds of questions, I know she is. I want them to have a way to find me, and I want them to know I'll answer those questions."

"You realize that they may destroy this letter first thing?" Mazelle asked.

"I know, but I'm hoping they read it first, and once they read it, they will remember if they ever need to know. At least I think they will." Liz blinked hard and then said, "We've talked a lot about choices these past few months, and you told me I can only control my own. So it is my choice to give them my name, and it is their choice what to do with the information. Right?"

"That's fair, I think," Mazelle said.

The next day Liz and her grandma packed the layette items into a box, put the letter on top, and tied it with twine in preparation for taking it to Anna's house to be delivered into the hands of the adoptive parents after the baby was born. They set aside a mint green gown, a little matching cap, a diaper for the newborn to wear, and a blanket to wrap her in.

That night, Liz dreamed about having her baby snatched from her arms. It was even worse than the nightmares she usually had about the night Drew broke up with her, or the ghastly war dreams of him being killed.

X

Endings & Beginnings

In the days that followed Belle's birth on February 22nd, Liz couldn't control her crying. She did not know where so many tears came from. Every day she stumbled out of bed and forced herself to get dressed, and together she and her grandma found a project to keep them occupied. They did jigsaw puzzles, played checkers, and went for walks. They sorted buttons and rearranged the fabrics in the sewing room closet. They made soup, bread and pie, and invited Anna for supper. They cleaned the attic, the basement, and the house. And through it all, Liz cried.

"What am I going to do?" she sobbed.

"You are going to cry all that pain out and get up every day and keep trying. One day it will get easier," Mazelle said bravely, fighting back her own tears. Clinging desperately to her grandma's promise, Liz kept on keeping on, and by the end of March, though she still cried herself to sleep, she cried a little bit less during the day.

"Grandma?" Liz asked at breakfast during the first week of April. "Do you think I could stay here with you for awhile longer? I could help with the garden and things. Maybe I could get a part-time job of some kind."

"Of course you can," Mazelle replied. "You're welcome to stay as long as you like."

"I thought I might take a few classes this fall. I need to figure out what to do with my life, and Northern Montana College is right here…" Her voice trailed off and she stared out the window of the kitchen.

"I think that's a very good idea," Mazelle encouraged.

"I have some money saved because I was planning to go to secretarial school like Mom did," Liz explained. "I've been thinking about being a teacher."

"I think it is worth a try, Liz," Mazelle agreed. At this point, she thought any goal that kept Liz from thinking about giving up her baby would be a good thing. The following week, Liz enrolled in college and registered for classes for the summer session. She hadn't planned to do that. The advisor suggested it, and faced with endless days of heartache, she decided taking classes would give her something useful to do. For the next ten weeks, she attended class, worked on her homework and helped her grandma around the house and garden.

In mid-August, Liz retrieved the mail from the mailbox and wheeled her grandma's old bicycle up the driveway. She used the bike to go to and from her classes whenever the weather permitted, which had been just about every day. Of course that would change in the winter. The basket on the front was big enough for her books and her notebook, and it was less than two miles to campus, so it was an easy ride.

"Grandma!" Liz called as she opened the kitchen door. "You got a letter from Mom!" She handed it over as Mazelle came into the kitchen.

Dear Mom and Liz,

I hope you are surviving the heat. It has been so hot here I can barely breathe! This is just a short note to let you know the boys have finished up with baseball and swimming and we are coming to visit you before school starts. Expect us on Saturday's train.
Love,
Caro

"They are coming to see us!" Liz exclaimed, a wide smile on her face. "I can hardly wait, and it's Thursday, so only two more days. And they'll be here for my birthday!" Real smiles from Liz were rare, and Mazelle appreciated this one. On Saturday, she drove the old truck to the train station and met the train. The boys and the luggage went into the back while Mazelle and Liz's parents squeezed into the cab of the truck for the drive back to Mazelle's house where Liz waited excitedly to see them. Mazelle was happy to let Phil do the driving. Supper that evening was a happy meal with much talking and laughing.

Later in their room, Phil asked, "Does Liz look okay to you?"

"She looks older and her eyes are sad, but she's been through a lot, and I think she is getting herself put back together," Caroline replied thoughtfully. "It takes a long time."

"If anybody knows that, we do. I thought she looked older, too, and thinner."

"I'm really glad that she's started school," Caroline said, and Phil agreed.

Liz invited her parents to come with her when she went to register for fall classes and showed them around the campus. They invited Anna to come for dinner on the night they celebrated Liz's nineteenth birthday with fried chicken and mashed potatoes and an apple crisp with homemade ice cream. The next day, Phil said he needed to get back to work, so he boarded the train and returned to Shelby.

"Phil still has trouble spending much time here, doesn't he?" Mazelle asked her daughter as they tidied up the kitchen after supper.

"There are so many sad memories for him here. I'm not sure it was a good idea for us to move so soon after it happened. His bosses were just trying to be kind, and it was a promotion, but sometimes I wonder if it wouldn't have been better to stay here and work through the grief," Caroline replied.

"Well, at the time everyone did what they thought was the best thing," Mazelle replied. "Maybe it was good to get away so he could deal with the loss in smaller doses."

"Maybe," Caroline agreed. "I still miss them, and I only knew them for a few years. They were wonderful people." Both women were quiet for a few minutes remembering Phil's parents. Wyatt and Amanda Baxter had died when their pickup slid off a muddy road and rolled over. Caroline knew that grief could destroy a relationship, and she was grateful that she and Phil had loved their way through the dark days of losing first their unborn child and then his parents.

"Liz, how are you doing, really?" her mom asked. She and Liz were in the sewing room on the evening before she and the boys were to return to Shelby.

"Grandma says time will make things easier," Liz replied. "It is still hard, though. Maybe it always will be." Liz knew that she was not quite answering the question, but she didn't want to admit to her mother, or anyone else, for that matter, that she still cried herself to sleep nearly every night, then got up every morning and forced herself to do the next thing on her list, whether it was a school assignment or a project with her grandma. She knew she would never stop missing Belle, and she was beginning to think she would never get over losing Drew either. She was determined to become a teacher and take charge of her life.

"I'm so sorry I couldn't spend more time here with you," Caroline apologized.

"Mom, you have a job, a husband, and two other kids, of course you couldn't be here with me. Don't feel bad about that."

"Your experience brought back a lot of sad memories for me," Caroline said slowly. "I had to work through them again."

"What do you mean, Mom?"

"I got pregnant, too, right after I finished secretarial school."

"I didn't know that! Is that why you and Dad got married?"

"We were talking about getting married, like you and Drew, and when I found out I was expecting a baby, we set a date just a few weeks away and started making arrangements for the wedding. Then… I had a miscarriage."

"Oh, Mom."

"I didn't want to go through with the wedding. I wasn't pregnant anymore, so I told Phil he was off the hook."

"But you said you were planning to get married," Liz said puzzled.

"Yes, but I wasn't thinking very clearly. People don't think clearly when they're upset."

"I know," Liz said softly. "Believe me, I know."

"Your dad insisted we get married. He said we had planned on it before we knew about the pregnancy and he still wanted to marry me regardless."

"Did my pregnancy bring back memories for him, too?" Liz asked, and her mom nodded.

"He is a good man, and he loves deeply. He said sometimes he still thinks about that time and wonders what our first child would have been like. And so do I." Mother and daughter were both quiet for a moment. "So anyway, we went ahead with the wedding, but it wasn't exactly a happy occasion, as you can imagine." Caroline shook her head. "The whole first year of our marriage was a hard time for both of us."

"So me being pregnant reminded you of all that?"

"Yes, it did, but we managed to get through that dark time in our lives. Our parents helped a lot. That was actually when I learned to appreciate the wisdom that comes with age. I wish you could remember Grandma and Grandpa Baxter. They were so kind, and so wise."

"Did Grandma Mazelle and Grandpa Robby help, too?" Liz asked.

"Oh yes. Between the four of them, someone was always available if I needed to cry – and I cried a lot."

"I still cry a lot, too," Liz confessed. "I'm beginning to wonder if I'll ever stop."

"I think that is part of healing, honey."

"What else did they do to help?"

"They brought us meals or had us over to eat. And they encouraged us to talk to each other, and told us we would be stronger and our love would be deeper if we shared our troubles. They said we would be better parents because we would understand what precious gifts children were. Stuff like that. Not preachy, but comforting and wise."

"That's the way Grandma is with me, Anna, too. I didn't always appreciate it, though."

"We went on to have you and your brothers, and we think of you as the greatest blessings in our lives. Nothing can erase that first loss, but you can go on and be happy. I know that from experience. I wanted you to know that part of our history so you'd understand and have hope."

"I think the only thing worse than having to give a baby away would be to lose one. At least I can be reasonably sure that Belle is healthy and happy," Liz said. She did not really believe that she would be able to go on and be happy, but she did not admit that to her mother.

"Belle?" Caroline asked.

"Oh," Liz smiled sadly. "I always thought the baby was a girl, so I started calling her Belle, just to myself, you know. Grandma's middle name is Maybelle and Anna's full name is Annabelle, and between the two of them, they helped me a lot. Regardless of what her adoptive parents named her, she will always be Belle to me."

"I think that's very sweet, dear," her mom said with tears in her eyes. "Belle is my first grandchild, you know."

"I know," Liz whispered as she blinked back her own tears.

The weeks sped by as Liz continued with her classes during the day and helped her grandma with preserving the garden fruits and vegetables in the evenings and on weekends. She was starting to forge new friendships among some of the other young women in her classes. She and Mazelle spent the Christmas holiday in Shelby, traveling by train and returning to Havre on the day after New Year's so Liz could register for winter classes. She took extra credits during the winter, applied herself to her classes, and her grades reflected her efforts. She decided that she would be like Anna and focus on a career as a way to stay busy and to be productive and financially self-sufficient.

During the day, at least, she was starting to get excited about becoming an elementary school teacher. She still cried at night, her dreams a jumble of Drew, who didn't love her after all, and Belle who was lost to her forever.

In February, Liz became very quiet and spent more time in her room than usual. The day before Belle's first birthday, she and Mazelle were invited to Anna's house for supper.

"Grandma, I don't really feel like going tonight."

"I suspect you don't really feel like doing much of anything right now, Liz. But Anna is expecting us, and has prepared a meal. It would be rude not to show up," Mazelle said firmly.

"I suppose you're right." Liz sighed and went to get her coat, hat and boots.

Anna served them a supper of scrambled eggs with bits of bacon, onion and a hint of cheese, accompanied by homemade cinnamon rolls. The house smelled of cinnamon and fresh bread when they walked in, and for the first time in more than a week, Liz felt hungry.

"This is really good, Anna," she said with a small smile.

"Thank you, I often have breakfast for supper," Anna replied. She paused and then said,

"Liz, I know Belle's birthday is tomorrow and that has to make you sad." Liz nodded and looked down at her plate. "Sometimes, right at first, adoptive parents let me know how things are going." Liz looked up.

"You've heard from Belle's parents?" she asked eagerly. "How is she? Tell me! Please."

"They sent me a short letter. I will let you read it, but you need to understand that I won't be able to give you regular updates. This will probably be the only information you ever get. Okay?" Anna asked seriously.

"I understand," Liz said earnestly. "It is more than I ever hoped for, and I won't expect more, I promise." Anna pulled a single sheet of paper from her apron pocket and handed it across the table. Liz unfolded it with trembling fingers and read,

Dear Anna,

We can't thank you enough for helping us to adopt Belle. We decided to keep the name her mother had given her in honor of you and your friend, and we gave her the middle name Elizabeth to honor the sacrifice her mother made in giving her up.

As she nears her first birthday, Belle is a healthy happy little girl, with blonde hair and brown eyes. She says a few words and is starting to walk. If you are still in contact with her mother, please let her know that we kept her correspondence and promise to explain everything to Belle when she is old enough to understand.

The bottom of the letter had a ragged edge and Liz could tell that it had been torn so as not to reveal the names of the adoptive parents. She looked up with tears slipping down her cheeks.

"Thank you! I think about her all the time. I try not to, but I can't help it." Liz smiled through her tears. "Now I know she's okay. Can I keep this? Please?" Anna hesitated, glanced at Mazelle, and then nodded.

"You need to move on, dear. I let you read that so you'd know that your little girl is in a good home. You need to let her go," Anna said gently.

"I'm trying," Liz whispered. And she did try. When thoughts of Belle came to mind, she repeated over and over, out loud if she was alone and silently if there were other people around, "Belle is safe and loved. Belle is safe and loved. Belle is safe and loved." As she repeated that phrase, she formed a mental picture of her little girl as happy and healthy, and as the days passed, she cried a little less, at least about that. Somehow, using the same technique about Drew, did not work. She still missed him as if he'd broken up with her yesterday. And she didn't know if he was happy or healthy, or safe.

XI
Apologies & Explanations

Liz sank into her grandma's rocking chair on the porch and sighed. It was the end of May and classes were finished until summer session. She and Mazelle had just finished planting the garden and she was tired. It was a good kind of tired, and she wondered if she would be able to sleep tonight without dreaming. Grandma had gone in to clean up and then they would think about supper. She needed to bathe and change, too, but she closed her eyes for a minute and her thoughts turned to the news the whole country had rejoiced at earlier in the month.

The war was over at last. Her mind wandered to Drew, hoping that he was all right, and wondering when he would be coming home. Sternly, she reminded herself that she needed to get on with her life. She still thought about him entirely too much. She sighed and opened her eyes, then sat bolt upright and gasped in shock. Drew was standing in front of the porch as if she had conjured him. She blinked but he was still there, and he looked terrible. He leaned heavily on a cane and was very thin. He wore rumpled fatigues, there were dark circles under his eyes, and he had several days' growth of beard on his face. He was staring at her with a grim intensity that she found unnerving.

Drew had spotted Liz sitting in the rocking chair well before he arrived at the porch. She was wearing overalls over a pink shirt and there was a smudge of dirt on her face. She was more beautiful than he remembered. At first he thought she was sleeping, but just as he stopped in front of the porch, she opened her eyes and sat up straight, all the color draining from her face. For a minute they stared at each other and then they both spoke at the same time.

"What are you doing here?"

"Lizzie, please, I need to talk to you. I made a terrible mistake!"

At that exact moment, Mazelle came through the door carrying two glasses of iced tea. She stopped when she saw Drew, glanced from his stark expression to Liz's shocked face and recovering quickly, she said, "Hello, Drew. Come and sit on the porch and have some iced tea." She motioned him to the chairs on the porch and waited for him to comply with her directive, which he did with his eyes still locked on Liz. Mazelle handed him one of the glasses, gave the other glass to Liz and said over her shoulder as she went back into the house.

"You'll stay for supper, of course. Everything will be ready in a few minutes."

"Lizzie," Drew began, but Liz interrupted him as she glared at the door where her grandmother had just disappeared.

"I'll show you the bathroom so you can get cleaned up." She stood abruptly, led him to the downstairs bathroom and got out clean towels. Then she went into the kitchen.

"Why did you invite him to supper?" she asked in a fierce whisper.

"He's a wounded soldier. He fought for our country. It's suppertime. I wouldn't feel right turning him away."

"I don't want him here!" Liz said angrily. "But I guess it's your house!"

"That is true, but don't you think you should to talk to him?"

"I don't have anything to say to him." There was a tremor in Liz's voice.

"He's here, and he says he wants to talk to you," Mazelle replied trying to speak calmly. "I think you should listen, but that's up to you, of course."

"He didn't want me, and I had to give up my baby," Liz said in an anguished whisper.

"I know, dear, but I heard him say he'd made a terrible mistake. People make mistakes."

"Fine." Liz snapped, then went upstairs to take a bath and change out of her gardening clothes.

"Lord," Mazelle whispered, alone in the kitchen, "I could sure use some of that wisdom old people are supposed to have in abundance." Then she set about augmenting the simple soup supper she had planned for herself and Liz with hearty ham and cheese sandwiches, thankful that there was leftover rhubarb pie for dessert.

Liz had not come downstairs yet when Drew reappeared bathed, shaved, and wearing a set of fatigues that were wrinkled, but clean. He still looked pale and drawn and there was a haunted look in his eyes. Mazelle wondered if that look was because of the war, or because of Liz. Not her business, she decided with a sigh.

"We have a bunkhouse in the barn, if you need a place to stay tonight," she said.

Drew looked relieved and said he'd appreciate that, so she gathered clean bedding and led him out to the bunkhouse so he could stow his things. It wasn't really a bunkhouse, just a corner of the old barn, but Robby had turned it into a cozy room with two beds, a small table and a tiny bathroom with a sink and toilet. It had been put to good use in the old days when Robby was running the farm and hired extra help for harvest. Mazelle cleaned it every spring and fall, so it was in good shape. By the time they got back, Liz had come downstairs wearing a denim skirt and a yellow blouse, and her damp hair was tied at the nape of her neck. The three of them sat down to eat. Liz didn't utter a word, so Mazelle engaged Drew in conversation.

"Are you on leave, Drew?"

"No. I caught some fragments from a mortar shell and had to have surgery on my leg. I was supposed to have medical leave but when I got to New York they told me that I was getting a medical discharge. I didn't ask for details, I was just glad to be done," Drew explained. "Don't get me wrong, I had a duty to serve my country, and I wouldn't shirk that, but war really is hell, and I'm glad it's over."

"So you've been on the train for several days?" Mazelle asked. Drew nodded.

"How did you know I was here?" Liz asked, abruptly, speaking for the first time. She had kept her eyes fixed on her soup bowl, though she had done more stirring than eating.

"I called home and asked Trish. She said you were staying with your grandma. I came here with you for the 4th of July the year I graduated, remember? So I took a chance." When Liz did not reply, he added, softly. "If you hadn't been here, Lizzie, I would have kept looking until I found you." Liz did not answer, or look at him, and Mazelle covered the awkward moment by getting up to retrieve the pie and a pot of tea.

"So you haven't been home yet?" Mazelle asked as she sat back down.

"No," Drew said. He opened his mouth as if he wanted to say more, and then changed his mind and applied himself to the pie. When he was finished he said, politely. "Thank you for supper, Mrs. Robins. It was the best meal I've had since I left home and I appreciate having a place to sleep, too." Liz looked startled by the second part of his statement.

"You're welcome, Drew," Mazelle said kindly. "You look tired enough to fall asleep standing up."

"Yes, ma'am, I am. If you don't mind, I think I will just go to bed," Drew said, and with a last glance at Liz, who still hadn't looked at him, he left the house, leaning heavily on his cane. When she was sure he was gone, Liz turned to her grandmother. "He's staying in the bunkhouse?" she asked incredulously. Mazelle nodded.

Liz stood up and began to clear the table, her movements abrupt and angry. She dried the dishes as Mazelle washed them, and went up to her room without another word.

Mazelle glanced at the clock, saw that it wasn't yet nine and went to the wall phone beside the refrigerator. Caroline answered on the third ring.

"Caro, we had an interesting evening here."

"What happened, Mom?"

"Drew showed up just before suppertime."

"He did? Is Liz okay? Tell me everything."

Mazelle told her daughter all that had transpired since she carried two glasses of iced tea out to the porch and discovered Liz and Drew staring at each other.

"I'm surprised he got off the train, not knowing for sure if Liz was there. He's the one who broke up with her, after all," Caroline said when Mazelle had finished.

"I heard him say he made a mistake. I think he still loves her. And the poor boy looks terrible in all senses of the word."

"What a mess!" Caroline exclaimed.

"Life can get messy, we know that." Mazelle sighed.

"Yes I know, and I can't shelter my children from life's problems. I wish I could, though. So, what's your plan for tomorrow?"

"I thought I'd go spend some time with Anna so Liz and Drew can have their discussion without any more interference from an old lady."

"You are not old, Mom."

"Today I feel old," Mazelle retorted. "I've been more than a little worried about Liz even before today. Last week she said she might look for a job in Havre after she finishes school and just live here with me. I said I enjoyed having her, but didn't she want to be with her friends, and with time, get married and have a family and she said no."

"She did?" Caro thought about that for a minute. "I thought she was spending some time with girls her own age at school and meeting new people."

"Oh, she participates in a study group now and then, but she doesn't go out at all. I think she is still in love with Drew, but giving up the baby, well, that's a huge stumbling block."

"Do you think she'll be able to tell him?"

"I don't know. She never talks about it. Not ever. And I suspect she still cries about it at night, because most mornings her eyes are red and puffy."

"Well, let me know how things go tomorrow, okay, Mom?" Caroline said, and Mazelle said she would.

Liz had not expected to get much sleep after the shock of seeing Drew, but an afternoon of working in the garden after a week of finals had taken its toll and she had gone right to sleep and slept without dreaming, for a change. Making her way downstairs, she found a note on the kitchen table that her grandma had gone to visit Anna and expected to be gone until noon.

"Great," Liz muttered to herself as she made tea and toast. She was not looking forward to any kind of discussion with Drew. As that thought crossed her mind, Drew knocked at the kitchen door. She crossed the room and opened it, standing back to let him in.

"Good morning, Lizzie."

Liz closed the door, and without her grandma there to run interference, she tried to be polite. "Is tea and toast okay for breakfast?"

"Yes," Drew replied. "Thank you."

Liz busied herself making more toast and pouring another cup of tea. She got the homemade raspberry jam out of the refrigerator, put everything on the table and sat down across the table from Drew, her hands clenched in her lap, her eyes fixed on her toast, and her appetite completely gone.

"I'm sorry, Lizzie, I really am." When Liz didn't look up or respond, Drew took a deep breath and continued, "Breaking up with you was the worst mistake I've ever made. But I never stopped loving you. I'm asking you to forgive me and to give me have another chance."

Liz struggled for words and finally choked out, "I can't!"

"You can't forgive me, or you can't give me another chance?" Drew asked carefully. It was Liz's turn to take a deep breath.

"I forgave you a long time ago," she said, her voice barely above a whisper. "But it's been two years. We can't be together now."

"Lizzie, I love you. I've loved you since I was sixteen years old," Drew said desperately.

"That's exactly what I said to you the night you broke up with me!" Liz retorted angrily.

"I know. I made a terrible mistake. I've regretted it every single day. It just wasn't something I could apologize for in a letter, and I couldn't come to see you until now."

"I can't!"

"Did you fall in love with someone else, is that it?" Drew pressed.

Liz shook her head frantic to keep her tears from falling. "No," she choked out.

"I love you, Lizzie, I want to marry you," Drew said, his voice was shaking. Liz stood up, the tears she had been trying to blink back were now streaming down her face.

"I told you – I can't!" she cried and she ran out of the kitchen and up the stairs. Drew sat at the table for a long time, but Liz didn't come back downstairs. At last, he walked out to the bunkhouse, gathered his things and walked back to the train station.

Mazelle returned from Anna's only to find two full teacups and two plates of toast, all untouched. Obviously, things had not gone well. Slowly she climbed the stairs and tapped on Liz's door. There was no answer, so she opened the door and peeked in, saw Liz asleep on the bed, then closed the door and went back downstairs to call her daughter and update her.

Liz slept for over an hour and woke with a headache. She did not mention Drew, nor did Mazelle.

When Drew got off the train in Shelby, he waited the half hour or so for the disembarking passengers to get their luggage and be on their way, and for the new passengers to board. When the train pulled out of the station, he sought out Phil Baxter.

"I need to talk to you and Mrs. Baxter. Please, it's important," he said.

"I'm going home in a few minutes. If you want to wait, you can ride with me."

"Thank you," Drew said, and while he waited he called the farm and asked Trish if she could pick him up in an hour or so.

Phil called Caroline to let her know that he was bringing Drew home with him, finished up his paperwork and led Drew to his car. The short ride to the Baxter house was silent and tense. When they were seated in the living room, Drew finally spoke.

"Did you know that I stopped in Havre to see Lizzie?" Liz's parents both nodded. "I know I did a really stupid thing when I broke up with her, then I didn't know how to fix things. I started a hundred letters trying to explain and apologize, but, well, I needed to be face to face for something like that." Drew clenched his fists on his thighs and continued, "I told her I was sorry and asked her for another chance and she just kept saying 'I can't' and she won't talk to me, or even look at me."

"I'm not sure what it is that you want from us, Drew." Phil said tersely. "Or from Liz. You two were talking about marriage, and then you left her high and dry. I really don't blame her for not wanting to talk to you."

"I'm sorry, so very sorry. I came to apologize to both of you for being such an idiot," Drew said.

"It isn't us you should be apologizing to, Drew," Caroline said. "Liz is the one you hurt."

"I know. I've told her how sorry I am, and I'll tell her again, because I'm not giving up. I'll do whatever it takes. I never stopped loving her." Drew insisted. "And I just wanted you to know what's going on and where I stand. Thanks for hearing me out."

Drew left soon after, and Phil and Caroline continued the discussion.

"What do you think?" Phil asked.

"I believed him when he said he still loves her. Mom thinks Liz still loves him, too. But they have a lot to talk about if they are going to work things out."

On Friday, Liz received a package in the mail. It had a Shelby postmark, so she assumed it was from her mother and opened it eagerly. It was from Drew. The package contained a notebook with a letter on top.

Dear Lizzie,

I'm sending you my journal because it's the only way I can think of to explain to you what the last two years have been like for me, and why I did what I did. I'm begging you to read it, and then I'm hoping we can talk. We used to be able to talk about anything, and I want to know what the last two years have been like for you.

I haven't given up on us. I love you and want to spend the rest of my life with you. I'll be coming back to Havre to see you next weekend.
All my love,
Drew

Mazelle returned from her book club meeting to find Liz sitting on the couch staring into space, the notebook and letter on her lap and the mailing envelope on the floor at her feet.

"What's that, Liz?" she asked. Wordlessly, Liz handed her the letter. When she had finished reading, she said, "Are you planning to read his journal?"

"Why should I?" Liz demanded crossly. She closed her eyes and rubbed her forehead. "I'm trying to get on with my life, and I'm having enough trouble as it is. Some days I feel like I'm hanging on to my sanity by a thread. I just can't deal with all this again. It hurts too much!" Her face was pale and her voice shook.

Mazelle knew this was hard, but she couldn't keep quiet when she thought Liz was doing the wrong thing. "Don't you think you have a moral responsibility to tell Drew about the baby?"

"No, I don't! I know there was a war and he had to do what he had to do, I get that," Liz snapped. "But why did I have to give up my baby?" She answered her own question. "Because Drew left me! Nothing changes that. It's hopeless!"

"Nothing is hopeless," Mazelle replied. "I agree that you can't go back to the way things were, but perhaps you can talk this through and go on."

"I don't want to talk about it! What's the point?" Liz stalked out of the room, and Mazelle shook her head sadly as she slipped the journal and Drew's letter back into the mailing envelope and laid it on the bottom stair. Liz ignored the envelope when she came downstairs for a bowl of soup after Mazelle had gone to bed. She hesitated on her way back upstairs, then reluctantly picked it up and carried it to her room. She wished she hadn't opened the package. She wouldn't have if she'd realized it was from Drew. But now it called to her, and reluctantly, she flipped it open.

The first entry was dated the day after Drew had broken up with her.

I didn't sleep at all last night. It just about killed me to break up with Lizzie, but I didn't know what else to do. Grandpa Joe told me how Dad went off to war and his girlfriend found someone else while he was gone. I told him Lizzie wasn't like that and that we loved each other. Then Grandpa Joe asked if I thought it was fair to ask Lizzie to wait for me when I might be gone for years, and I might not even come back at all, because that's how war is. Sometimes people die. When he put it like that, I felt selfish. Now I just feel sick. I can't forget the look on Lizzie's face and I can still hear her crying.

The next entry was dated a week later.

Basic training is tough, and I'm glad because at least while we are training, I can block out the mess I've made with Lizzie. I tried several times to write a letter and apologize and explain, but I just couldn't find the words. And a part of me can still hear Grandpa Joe's question - what if I'm gone for years or don't come back at all? I decided this journal will be a letter from my heart to hers. If I don't survive, maybe these pages will find their way to her and she will understand that I never stopped loving her.

The rest of the entries started with "Dear Lizzie" and were written like letters, telling her what he was doing and how much he missed her. He wrote often, but not daily, describing the other men in his unit and their training activities. Some of the men had wives or girlfriends back home with whom they exchanged letters. Now and then one of the girlfriends sent a "Dear John" letter, but most of the letters the men received were upbeat and encouraging and full of news from home. He told how the other soldiers read and re-read those letters, sometimes sharing a portion of them out loud. The descriptions of Drew's combat experiences were brief and general, but there was enough detail for Liz to get a feel for how awful the reality of war was and how it affected him, especially when there were casualties. He speculated about what she was doing, assuming that she had gone to secretarial school as she had planned to do. Drew ended each entry with a comment that his belief in their love was all that got him through each day and how he hoped and prayed she felt the same way.

Liz read through the night, finishing the journal as the sun started to peek through her window. As she sat there watching the sunrise, she felt hope flicker in her heart, and she knew what she had to do. She got up and went downstairs to talk to her grandma.

"I'm sorry I was rude to you yesterday." She apologized as she fixed her tea. While she had breakfast, she explained what she had read in Drew's journal.

"I guess I can understand how he thought he was being noble, even when he was being an idiot." Liz commented. Mazelle listened attentively, but didn't say much. She had encouraged Liz to do the right thing, but now it was up to her to work through the details on her own.

Liz thought about Drew's journal at odd times during the day and re-read parts of it in the evenings before she went to bed. Drew arrived the next weekend, as he had promised, and was pleased when Liz met his gaze and told him she had read his journal.

"Thank you," Drew said, with relief. "Is there anything you want to ask me about it?"

"After reading about what your Grandpa Joe said happened to your dad, I can understand why you thought you needed to break up with me."

"I can't blame Grandpa Joe, Lizzie. He was there when my dad went through that experience, and he was just trying to make me aware of some of the problems war causes in people's lives," Drew hastened to explain. "I made my own decision. I know now that it wasn't a good decision, but I made it."

"I don't blame your grandpa, either." Liz agreed. She knew this was the moment to tell him about Belle. "Drew," she said hesitantly. "We've both changed a lot in the last two years." Drew watched her face change to a serious expression, and he tensed, afraid that she was about to tell him none of it mattered, that it was too late, and that she didn't want to see him anymore.

"All I'm asking for is another chance, Lizzie." Drew said quickly, before she could send him away. "How about if we just spend some time together and get re-acquainted?"

"Okay," she agreed, and he sighed in relief. That weekend they attended a movie, went out for ice cream, took a couple of long walks and spent time on the porch sipping iced tea and chatting with Mazelle. When it came time for Drew to catch the train to Shelby, Liz still hadn't found a way to tell him what he needed to know. On an impulse, she ran upstairs, retrieved the envelope Drew had used to mail his journal to her, replaced his journal and added her own, then resealed it and took it downstairs.

"Here is your journal. Thanks for letting me read it," she said as she handed it to him. He slipped it into his bag then reached out and caressed her cheek.

"So I'll come back next weekend?" he asked.

"If you want to," she replied, not quite meeting his eyes.

Drew took the train to Havre the next two weekends in a row and spent time with Liz. They got along fine, but Drew went home with an uneasy feeling that he was missing something. He mulled things over but simply could not figure out what was wrong. On Wednesday, he was pacing around his room in frustration when he saw the envelope he had used to mail his journal to Lizzie. He opened it to put his journal away, and found Liz's journal alongside his own. Wondering why Liz hadn't said anything, he sat on the bed and started to read. Each of the entries was dated, and it looked like Liz had written nearly every day. The first entry was from the end of June.

Drew's throat got tight as he read of Liz's pain and bewilderment, and her conclusion that after he'd gotten what he wanted, he didn't want to marry her anymore. He skimmed through her preparations for the trip to Havre and several weeks of general entries about things she and her grandma did together. Then he read an entry from October, and his mind froze.

> *I felt the baby kick tonight, and that made every-thing real. I realized I've been trying not to care too much, but when I felt that little bump, I knew I was already in love with this baby.*

Drew read the entry three times, his hands shaking and his heart pounding. Pregnant! Liz had been pregnant and he hadn't even suspected. Why hadn't she told him? Why hadn't he asked? He was an idiot! He went back to the first entry and started again, reading more carefully this time, and because he was looking for clues, he caught nuances he had missed the first time. On the twenty-first of February she wrote that she was in labor. The next entry said that Belle had been born on the 22nd of February. Regular entries did not begin again until April, and they were stilted and lifeless, simply listing the details of her life as if she were going through the motions without caring one way or the other.

Liz made note of Belle's first birthday, and included the partial letter written by the adoptive parents to Anna. After that, the entries slowly perked up. Reading them, Drew could almost feel Liz pulling herself together by sheer force of will. It was morning when Drew came to the last entry.

> *Drew is home from the war and he says he nev-er stopped loving me. He gave me his journal to read. (It is odd that both of us started a journal about the same time.) Reading it helped me under-stand what went on in his life the past two years. War must be awful. I know I have to figure out a way to tell him about Belle. We can't be together with that between us, but it still hurts so much I can't talk about her without crying. What if I tell him that I gave our baby away, and he hates me for it?*

His heart ached for her, and he blinked away tears, as he realized why she hadn't spoken of this heartache, especially to him. He set Lizzie's journal aside and went upstairs to ask his dad for a ride to the train.

The trip from Shelby to Havre was both the longest and the shortest train ride of Drew's life. On the one hand, he could hardly wait to get there and talk to Lizzie, and on the other, he was afraid he would say or do the wrong thing. He paced from one train car to the next, trying to figure out what to say and how to say it to convince Lizzie to give them another chance.

Liz lay in bed staring at the ceiling, not wanting to get up. Each day that passed brought the weekend closer, and Drew said he was coming to see her again. She could tell he hadn't read her journal; he probably hadn't even found it. That was her fault for being such a coward. She should have just handed it to him as he left that day, instead of hiding it. Honestly, she thought in disgust, she was surrounded by strong women and she was the weakest little ninny she had ever met. Her life was a mess, and all she did was make it worse. She hated being such a crybaby. Her anger and frustration got her out of bed and dressed. She resolved to tell Drew about Belle when he came to see her on Friday.

Mazelle was rolling out pie dough when Liz entered the kitchen. She looked up and frowned in concern. "What's wrong, dear?"

"Oh, nothing. I didn't sleep very well and woke up with a headache. You're making pie?"

"I felt like baking today. Maybe you should have a cup of tea and lie down for awhile to see if you can get rid of the headache," Mazelle suggested.

"I need to return some books to the library. A walk might help." After tea and toast, Liz put her books in a bag and set off for the campus library. Once there, she browsed the shelves and chose a couple of new books to read. She met a classmate and chatted for a few minutes, so it was mid-afternoon before she started to walk back. She heard the train whistle when she was almost home and sighed. She needed to figure out what to say to Drew tomorrow. She climbed the stairs to bathe and change as soon as she got home, enjoying the aroma of apple pie that permeated the house. She had just stepped onto the porch to sit in the rocking chair when she saw Drew.

"What are you doing here?" she gasped in surprise.

"Lizzie, my love, that's what you said the first time I found you on this porch."

"But it's only Thursday." She stared at him perplexed.

"I read your journal." Drew said with his eyes locked on hers as he stepped up onto the porch and reached for her hands. "I'm so sorry, Lizzie. So sorry for everything you had to go through by yourself."

She started to cry, and he pulled her into his arms. "I had to give away our baby girl!" she sobbed, two years worth of grief and anger pouring out with her tears.

"I know, it's my fault," he murmured into her hair. "I'm sorry, Lizzie, I'm so sorry." He blinked back tears of his own as he held her. When Liz finally quieted, Drew led her to the porch swing and they sat down. Turning to face her, he took both her hands in his. Looking into her eyes, he chose his words carefully.

"Fighting in a war was awful, but what you went through was awful, too, maybe even worse. And it was my fault, Lizzie. If I hadn't broken up with you, we'd have gotten married and things would have been a lot different." He took a deep breath. "I know we can't change that, but we can go on from here together. I want to do that, Lizzie. I want that more than anything. I love you. I want us to get married and have a family and get old together. I'll wait if you aren't ready, but that's what I want." Lizzie searched his face for a long moment.

"Grandma said that, too. That we can't go back or change anything, I mean, but that maybe we could go forward. I want that, too, Drew. I couldn't stop loving you, either."

"Couldn't?" Drew asked. "Did you try, Lizzie?" She nodded. "I'm lucky you couldn't, then." Drew said with a sigh of relief. He wished he'd brought the ring with him, or flowers, but he'd thought only of getting here. He had to ask her right now. The words burst from him in a rush.

"Will you marry me, Lizzie?" he asked. She looked startled, but only for a moment, and then she smiled.

"Yes!"

"Thank God!" Drew exclaimed. "Let's not wait, Lizzie. We've already wasted two years!"

XII

Making Plans & Mending Fences

The two young people were sitting on the porch swing, discussing wedding dates when Mazelle returned from visiting Anna. She noticed Liz's tear-stained face and Drew's arm around her shoulders at the same time.

"Don't mind me, I'm just going in to fix supper."

"You can be the first to congratulate us," Drew assured her, looking up with a happy smile. "Lizzie has just agreed to marry me!"

"Congratulations!" Mazelle exclaimed. "I love weddings!" She was so relieved that these two finally seemed to be on the same page. Honestly, she had begun to wonder if they were ever going to sort things out.

"I want to call Mom, and then I'll help with supper," Liz said as she stood up and went off to the kitchen to use the phone.

"I remember Liz saying you were going to take over your dad's farm, is that right?" Mazelle asked, lingering on the porch.

"Yeah," Drew replied. "That was the plan before the war. Since I've been back I've been focused on getting things straightened out between me and Lizzie, so I haven't really been much help to him, and to tell you the truth, he doesn't seem to need me."

"Maybe he just wanted to give you some time."

"Maybe. But lately I've been wondering if he just offered to let me run the farm when I graduated because that's what Grandpa Joe did for him. The thing is, Grandpa Joe doesn't love farming like my dad does, he just did it to make a living."

"I see," Mazelle said. "So do you have a passion for farming?"

"No," Drew admitted. "I'm more like Grandpa Joe. I like the work, and the lifestyle, but..."

"Do you know what you would rather do?" Mazelle asked.

"I might want to farm, eventually, but I'd kinda like to go to college, and maybe learn a trade, too, or, well I guess I don't really know for sure. But I know that if I go back to the farm, Lizzie either wouldn't get to finish school, or we'd have to live apart. I don't like either options."

"You've already done some thinking about this, haven't you?" Mazelle asked.

"I've had a lot of time to think, sitting on the train for several hours every weekend." Drew shrugged. "I had to focus on something positive to keep from going insane."

"If you decide, after talking to Liz and your parents, of course, that you want to go to school, you and Liz are more than welcome to live here," Mazelle offered.

"Thanks very much. I'll talk to Lizzie about it and see what she says. I could be your hired man for the bigger chores around here to help pay our way."

Mazelle shook her head and smiled, her eyes twinkling. "When you marry Lizzie, you'll become my grandson, so rest assured that I'll boss you around a lot more because of that than if you were the hired man," she teased. "And you can start calling me Grandma right away," she added.

"It's a deal!" Drew said, and held out his hand to shake. They were laughing and shaking hands when Liz reappeared.

"What's so funny, Grandma?" Liz asked.

"I was just telling Drew that since he's going to be my grandson, he can call me 'Grandma' and I'll start bossing him around. Shall we go inside and get supper on the table?" While they ate, Liz said that her mother had suggested that she come home with Drew on the train and stay a week or so. She thought they could get together with Drew's mom and start planning the wedding. Liz asked Mazelle to come, too, and on Sunday afternoon, the three of them boarded the train for Shelby. Drew was happy to have things settled with Lizzie, but was also dreading the conversation he knew he must have with his parents as soon as he got home.

"Drew? What's wrong dear?" his mother asked, frowning at him in concern. "You've hardly touched your supper."

Drew quit pretending to eat and put his fork down. "I have some things to tell you about Lizzie and me."

Trish looked up. She lived in town, but usually came to the farm for Sunday dinner with her parents. "Liz wouldn't be my friend anymore because you broke up with her."

"Sorry, sis," said Drew. "But there was another reason why she did that."

"Tell us, son," said John. Drew began by explaining why he'd broken up with Liz before he left. "I'm sorry my dad told you that old story, because it turned out to be one of those blessings in disguise for me. If my high school girlfriend hadn't found someone else, I'd never have married your mother, and she's the best thing that ever happened to me."

Jean touched his hand and smiled, a little surprised at the quiet declaration from her usually taciturn husband.

"I knew Lizzie wasn't the kind of girl who would cheat on me while I was gone, Dad. What I couldn't get out of my mind was that I might not come back at all." His father nodded in understanding. "And there's more." Drew explained that Lizzie had been pregnant with his child, and that he hadn't known. His voice shook as he told how she'd gone to stay with her grandma, had the baby, and given the little girl up for adoption. He stopped to a take deep breath and steady his voice.

"Liz had your baby?" Jean asked, shocked. Drew nodded. "And gave her up for adoption?" Drew nodded again, his eyes fixed on his mother's face. Trish was also in shock, repeating her mother's words.

"But she should have told you!" Jean wailed. "And us!"

"Mom, think about it," Drew said as gently as he could. "I basically told her to find a new boyfriend and then I left. Lizzie thought I had stopped loving her."

"But, Drew, that was your baby, too, and our grandchild! We should have been told, whether the two of you were together or not."

"Maybe so, Mom," Drew said grimly. "But the reason Lizzie didn't try to contact me was because she thought I didn't love her anymore. Everything that happened after I broke up with her was my fault. Not Lizzie's – mine. I'm the one you should be upset with."

"Poor, Liz!" Trish murmured. "And she couldn't talk to me about it because I'm your sister." She had immediately put herself in Liz's shoes and wondered what she would have done in the same situation. She glared at Drew. "Are you going to be able to fix this?" But Drew's attention was fixed on his mother and he didn't answer.

"I need to know that there won't be a problem between our family and Liz over the baby we all lost," he said. "Please, Mom, we can't go back and change anything."

"It just wasn't right what she did," Jean insisted with tears in her voice.

"I think Liz did the best she could," John said. He touched Jean's shoulder and added. "That's all we can ask of anyone, isn't it?"

"Yeah," Trish nodded. "She didn't have a lot of choices." The three of them turned toward Jean. She looked around the table with tears in her eyes.

"But we have a grandchild we didn't even know about!" she said in an anguished whisper as she dabbed at her eyes with her napkin.

"Can you try to get past it, Mom? I know you are angry, but it will ruin the future for Lizzie and me if you can't," Drew pleaded. There was silence around the table as Jean struggled with her answer.

"I'll try, Drew," Jean said finally. "I do understand that it was hard for Liz, and you know I've always loved her, so I'll try." Drew slumped in relief. He knew his mother, and she would do as she had promised.

"You didn't answer my question. Are you going to be able to fix this with Liz?" Trish wanted to know.

"That's what I've been trying to do since I got back. Lizzie and I finally talked about everything this weekend. I asked her to marry me." Jean looked up.

"What did she say?" Trish demanded.

"She said 'yes'" Drew replied, with a worried glance at his mother, adding "We want to get married right away, on September first, so they want to get together and plan the wedding next week."

Jean closed her eyes and wondered how she could be happy and sad and upset all at the same time.

The Baxter family enjoyed the 4th of July festivities on Wednesday and celebrated Grandma Mazelle's birthday on Thursday. On Friday, Caro, Mazelle and Liz drove out to the Edwards farm for a wedding planning session and lunch. While her mother and grandma were exchanging greetings with Jean Edwards, Liz slipped downstairs and knocked on Trish's bedroom door. All the bedrooms in this old farmhouse were in the basement where they stayed cool in the summer and warm in the winter. The last time she'd been here the walls in Trish's room were off-white and adorned with photographs. There had been a patchwork quilt on the bed, bookcases crammed with books, and bits of memorabilia taped around the edges of the mirror. She wondered if any of that had changed, now that Trish had an apartment in town.

"I'm sorry, Trish," Liz said as soon Trish opened the door.

"It's okay," Trish answered promptly. "I know why you couldn't be around me." She stepped forward and engulfed Liz in a fierce hug. "I'm so sorry about the baby, Liz," she whispered.

"Me, too," Liz murmured, swallowing past the familiar ache that tightened her throat whenever she thought about Belle. "Thanks for understanding. You know, I was almost as upset about losing you as a sister as I was about Drew being gone." She shrugged and added, "And I didn't know if you would be able to forgive me."

"Well, now that my idiot brother finally got things straightened out and we are truly going to be sisters, let's forget the bad stuff and get to the good stuff, okay?" Trish said.

"Okay," Liz agreed, relieved. Then she said, anxiously, "Would you be my maid of honor? I don't want anybody else."

"I'd love to!" Trish said with a big smile, and the two of them hugged again. "We need to get together and catch up. I've missed you!"

"I've missed you, too!" Liz looked down at the floor. "Um, does your mom hate me? You know, because I didn't tell anyone about being pregnant?"

"It made her angry, and sad," Trish replied soberly. "It might take her a little time to work through it, but she doesn't hate you. I don't think my mom could hate anyone!" The two friends made their way up the stairs, where Liz went directly to Jean.

"I'm sorry," she said, "I didn't mean to hurt…" But before she could say another word, however, Jean embraced her.

"I think I'll always be sad about the baby, Liz, but I am happy about the wedding."

"Me, too." Liz replied, thankful that Jean was making the effort to forgive her and well aware that it would take time. The women got busy with wedding plans, adhering to Liz's desire for a small family wedding with garden flowers for the church and the bouquet, church clothes for the wedding party, and a basic cake and coffee reception after the ceremony. Caroline volunteered to get the invitations, and Jean agreed to make arrangements for the cake and the reception. As they talked Liz looked around the table and realized she was blessed to have these women in her life.

While the ladies were meeting in the kitchen, Drew wandered out to the barn where he found his dad cleaning his workbench. John was meticulous about his tools.

"Hey Drew, did the wedding talk get to you?" John smiled.

"Yeah, I had to get out of there. Plus I needed to talk to you anyway."

"What's on your mind?"

"Well, I've had a lot of time to think on the train, and I've been thinking that maybe we need to talk some more about me taking over the farm." Drew said, somewhat nervously. John paused, then resumed arranging his wrenches.

"Your mother said the same thing to me just this morning."

"She did?" Drew asked in surprise.

"Yup. Your mother is a smart woman, you know?"

"Believe me, I know! So, what did she say?"

"She said that I have a passion for farming and you don't know what your passion is yet. Well, except for Liz, of course. She said I'm not ready to give up farming and she won't be able to live with me if I retire before I'm ready." John grinned at Drew over his shoulder and then continued to arrange his tools.

"She said that?"

"Yup." John turned to face Drew.

"Well, good job, Dad! Now you can tell her we talked and that she was right. That will make her happy." Drew laughed, both relieved and amused. "And she *was* right, you know."

"She usually is. I don't know what I'd do without her." John smiled, leaning back against his workbench and crossing his arms. "So tell me exactly how she is right this time."

"Lizzie and I are planning to live with her Grandma Mazelle. Lizzie is just about finished with college, but it will take me four years, or so. Do you want to keep farming for awhile and talk about farming again when I'm through with school?"

"Sounds like a good plan to me. Glad that's settled then." He reached out to give Drew a one-armed hug.

At supper that evening, Liz looked around the table and said she had an announcement to make. Adam and John groaned.

"Is it more wedding stuff?" Adam asked, with an exaggerated sigh.

"Sort of." Liz grinned at both her brothers. "Actually, I have something to show you first and then something to tell you." She raised her left hand and displayed her engagement ring. Drew had finally found an opportunity to give it to her that day. He had explained that two years ago he had planned a romantic dinner and flowers, but now that she'd said yes, he just wanted his ring on her finger. When Caroline and Mazelle had gushed over the ring, her dad had smiled in approval, and her brothers had rolled their eyes. Liz told her parents that they would be living with Mazelle while Drew started college and she finished her studies.

"That's wonderful, dear!" her mom exclaimed.

"I'm glad you'll be able to finish college," Phil commented, "and this will give the men something to focus on while you ladies are occupied with the wedding. I'll need help from you two." He looked at his sons.

"What do we have to do?" John asked hesitantly.

"We have to load all of Drew and Liz's things up and take them to Grandma's house. It will probably take two trips. I'll need strong backs for all the lifting and carrying." Adam and John exchanged looks and grinned.

"We'll do anything to get out of wedding stuff." John vowed, and Adam nodded in agreement.

"I hadn't thought about moving our stuff, Dad. Thanks!" said Liz.

After supper, Adam went off to spend time with his buddies, John challenged his grandma to a game of checkers, and Phil sat down to read the weekly newspaper.

"You've accomplished quite a bit in a few days time. I have to admit that when you decided on September 1st for a wedding," Caroline said as they were doing dishes. "I thought it would be hard to get everything done."

"It helps that we both went to the same church growing up, and can have the wedding and the reception there," Liz agreed.

"How did Drew get a ring so fast?"

"He said it's been in his sock drawer since before I graduated," Liz said soberly. "He didn't stop loving me, Mom!"

"I'm so glad, dear. Have you thought about a dress?"

"Not yet, but that's the next thing on my list. What do you think?"

"It depends on what you want, I suppose. Mom made my dress, and you could probably wear that if you like the style. We're about the same size. Or we could make a dress for you, if we could find fabric."

"You still have your dress? I'd love to wear it. I've seen your wedding picture. I love that dress!"

They hurried to finish the dishes and then they went to retrieve the dress from the shelf of the closet. It was packed neatly in a box, wrapped in plastic. Liz slipped it on, and stood in front of the mirror while her mom fastened the buttons in the back.

"Oh, Mom, it's beautiful," she breathed. "And it fits."

"There's a tiara that belonged to Grandma Amanda, and the veil she made for me, too." Caroline lifted them from the box and held them up, then helped Liz try them on, too. "I'm going to see if Mom is finished with her checkers game, so she can see how you look." Mazelle appeared in the doorway a few moments later.

"You look beautiful, Liz," she said softly. "And you look a lot like your mother."

Liz glanced at her mother, then looked into the mirror again and whispered. "Do you think Belle will look like me?"

"Probably," Mazelle answered, and Caroline nodded in agreement.

"I'm sorry, I didn't mean to ruin the moment with sad thoughts, I just think of her at odd times." Liz said, blinking back tears.

"And you will all of your life," her mom warned. "She's a part of you. Don't apologize. Let it happen, think about her when she comes to your mind, pray that she's okay, and then go on. Right, Mom?"

"I think so, yes," Mazelle agreed. "You need to find a balance between focusing on Belle too much and trying to forget her entirely. Neither approach is healthy." Mazelle patted Liz on the shoulder. "Moving forward and living your life is healthy."

Liz and Mazelle were scheduled to return to Havre on the train on Sunday morning, so Saturday night they were all invited to supper at the Edwards farm. Mazelle and Caroline brought strawberry pies and potato salad. Jean made a pot of baked beans to go with the hot dogs and hamburgers on the grill.

Drew and Liz were returning from a walk after supper when Grandpa Joe called to them from the porch and then walked out to meet them. It looked like he had been waiting for them.

"I wanted to talk to you both." Joe said, looking over their heads at the sunset. "Sorry my loose talk caused you so much trouble."

"Grandpa, I already told you I made my own decision, and I don't blame you for pointing out the possibilities to me," Drew assured him, but Grandpa Joe's eyes were on Liz.

"I don't blame you either. Maybe we had to lose each other to appreciate each other. My grandma says everything happens for a reason. Anyway, we're together now, and that's what matters."

"You're sure?" Grandpa Joe asked.

"I'm sure," Liz replied. "I do have a question, though." Joe nodded. She looked earnestly into his lined face. "Is it okay if I call you Grandpa? Because I don't have a grandpa of my own, you know? And you've had a lot of experience."

Joe couldn't help but laugh. "Liz, my girl, it would be my pleasure to be your grandpa." He tipped his cap to her, said goodnight and was still smiling as he moved toward his pickup.

"And that is just one of the reasons I love you, Lizzie!" Drew said, giving her a hug and dropping a kiss on the top of her head. "He felt really bad, and I've talked to him and talked to him but nothing I said made him feel one bit better. You made him laugh. Amazing!"

August was a busy month. Liz's dad and brothers made two trips to move her and Drew's things to Havre. They were going to use her grandparent's old bedroom, so Liz had spent several evenings putting their clothes away. The rest of their things were stored in the bunkhouse to be dealt with later. When she and Drew registered for fall classes, Drew discovered that Congress had passed the G.I. Bill to help servicemen with school expenses, so he was completing the paperwork for that.

On the day before Liz's twentieth birthday, Mazelle and Liz took the train to Shelby. They enjoyed a birthday dinner and cake with her family and planned to spend the rest of the week taking care of last minute wedding preparations. On the day after Liz's birthday, she and Trish finally had a chance to catch up.

Liz asked if she'd gone to secretarial school as they had planned to do together, and Trish explained how when Drew got drafted and Liz left, she just didn't want to go off on her own.

"Great Falls is the biggest city in Montana and now the Air Base is there, so it seems even bigger. But I'm a country girl, and I just didn't feel like going to live there by myself."

"So when did you go then?" Liz asked.

"After harvest. Janet Brady, do you remember her? She was a year ahead of us. Anyway, she called and said she was halfway through a nurse's training program and her roommate quit school to get married. She said I could room with her."

"Perfect timing!" Liz commented.

"Exactly. Mom and Dad thought I needed a change, so they pretty much packed me up and took me and my stuff down there and dropped me off."

"Are you glad you went?"

"Yeah. I thought it was too late to register, so I was going to wait and go in January. I had to do a late registration the same day classes started, so things were hectic for a little bit, but once I got into a routine, it was fine."

"Well, I'm glad you went to school, and Janet was a real nice girl from what I remember."

"She's great. We got along really well and got to be pretty good friends. She was in a two-year program and mine was one year, so we finished at the same time."

"Let's get to the good stuff," Liz said. "Drew said you have a boyfriend."

"Actually, you know him," Trish replied. "It's Drew's friend, Luke Forrest. He'll be the best man at the wedding."

"Hold on! In my opinion, Drew will be the best man at the wedding," Liz scolded her friend teasingly.

"You're madly in love, so your opinions are suspect!" Trish retorted.

"I am madly in love, and it's a relief to finally be able to stop pretending that I'm not," Liz agreed seriously. "But back to Luke – tell me everything!"

"He got drafted the same time Drew did, but he got injured last year. It was pretty scary for awhile, he was in a coma and they thought he might die. I heard all about it at church. His mother was a wreck, as you can imagine. When he finally recovered from all his injuries, and I'm not even sure what they all were because he doesn't ever talk about it, he got a medical discharge and the army sent him home. I saw him in church, when he still looked pretty rough, pale and thin and using a cane."

"That's how Drew looked when he first got back," Liz said soberly. "Drew doesn't talk about it either."

"Neither does my dad, come to think of it," Trish said.

"So, tell me more about Luke."

"One day at church he asked me about Drew, but at that point Drew wasn't keeping in touch very well, so I didn't have much to tell him. He kept talking to me, though, and then one day he asked me out."

"You love him?" Liz asked.

Trish pushed a strand of dark brown hair behind her ear, a faraway look in her blue eyes. "War changes things, you know? It makes you think about things you might not have thought about before. I love him, and we are spending a lot of time together. I'm not sure he loves me, so we'll see how things go. It's only been a few months. If it's meant to be, it will happen, and if not, it won't," Trish said philosophically. "I want us both to be sure."

"Don't be afraid to hope, Trish, okay?"

"Okay, I won't. But I think taking some time is smart. You and Drew had three years before he went to war." Trish reminded Liz.

"Well yes, but we were kids then!"

"And now you are ancient and wise?" Trish said, with eyebrows raised. They laughed about that and then moved on to discussing the whereabouts of some of their other high school friends and what they were doing.

On the following Saturday, the wedding went off without a hitch and was well attended by family and close friends. Mazelle's son James and his wife Sandra were there from Great Falls, and their daughter Mary and her husband from Townsend. Mazelle's other son Pete and his wife Karen came, too, and their daughter Lucy and her husband the minister drove up from Wyoming. It was good to see all of them.

Mazelle was thrilled that Drew and Liz were going to be living with her, but she knew they would need some time alone. They didn't have the time or the money for a honeymoon, so Mazelle decided to stay in Shelby for an extra week or maybe two, to give them a chance to settle in at the house in Havre before their classes started. She was also entertaining the idea of going to visit her two sons and their families for the holidays, maybe spending Thanksgiving with one and Christmas with the other. She knew her life would change yet again with a young couple in the house, but then, things had changed when Liz came to stay with her, and that had turned out all right. Life was always changing and now that she was accustomed to having Liz live with her, she wasn't sure she would want to live alone again.

XIII

Time Flies

Liz and Drew quickly settled into their life as a married couple, helping Mazelle with the chores and attending classes. Drew wasn't sure what he wanted to do, so he took a variety of classes and quickly discovered that the ones he enjoyed the most involved the things he had done on the farm, like welding, auto mechanics, accounting, and basic carpentry. He used what he learned in the classroom to build on the experience he'd gained growing up and working with his dad and his grandpa on the family farm. As she had planned, Mazelle spent the holidays visiting her two sons in Great Falls and Helena. She'd been back for a few weeks when Drew took her aside.

"Something is wrong with Lizzie," he said worriedly.

"Why do you say that?" Mazelle hadn't noticed anything out of the ordinary.

"The past few days she's just gotten really quiet and she seems sad. Then last night she cried in her sleep. She said she just had a bad dream, but I don't think she was telling me the truth."

"Oh," Mazelle said in understanding. "Well, it's February, dear. Belle's birthday is coming up and I suppose it is natural that Liz would remember and be sad. This happened last year, too."

"I see," Drew said. He was relieved to know what was wrong, but suddenly sad, too, reminded of the daughter he hadn't known about until a few months ago. "This will be Belle's second birthday?"

"Yes," Mazelle confirmed.

That afternoon, on his way home from school, Drew stopped at a flower shop and bought two pink carnations in a white vase. He found Liz upstairs, gazing sightlessly out the window of their bedroom.

"I know you are thinking about Belle," he said from the doorway. Liz turned as he crossed the room and handed the vase to her. "Don't shut me out, Lizzie. Let's remember Belle's birthday together."

"Oh, Drew," Liz smiled through her tears. "I'm sorry. I can't seem to find a balance between remembering and forgetting."

"I know," Drew said as he held her close. "I guess it's another one of those things that takes time."

Over the next week or so, Liz pulled herself together and regained her equilibrium. And every year after that, Drew brought her a bouquet of pink flowers and they remembered together.

Mazelle accompanied Drew and Liz to Shelby at the end of May and they stayed for ten days. They celebrated Adam's high school graduation with the Baxter family and attended Trish and Luke's wedding the next weekend. It was a great chance to catch up with friends, neighbors and family.

"I knew you and Luke were perfect for each other!" Liz told Trish as they managed to spend some time together a few days before the wedding. Where are you going to live?"

"Great Falls. We just finished moving all of my things down there last week. Luke is going to school, and I have a job."

"Good for Luke!" Liz exclaimed. "What is he going to study, and when did he start school?"

"He wants to be a high school math teacher. He started last year, same time Drew did."

"Really?" Liz said. "I guess I assumed he would be a mechanic like his dad."

"He found out in the army that he has a knack for explaining things, he gets along good with kids, and he loved school. Then he found out about the G.I. Bill, so he decided to go for it."

"What about your job?"

"I start in two weeks, so we'll have a little time to settle in. We got an apartment where I can walk to work, and Luke can walk to school. He decided to go during the summer, too, so he can finish sooner."

"Maybe he can get a teaching job in Shelby," Liz said.

"That would be a dream come true for him, and I would like to live close to both sets of our parents, if that's possible. Luke would like to help Dad on the farm during the summer and teach the rest of the time. We'll see if that works out."

They already knew it had worked out for others. Most of the teachers in their community had another job during the summer. Their high school math teacher had an outdoor painting business, one of the English teachers did private tutoring, the science teacher and several others worked for local farmers, helping with seeding and harvest.

Liz spent the rest of the summer helping Mazelle with gardening and household chores, while Drew was in demand as extra help with several Havre area farmers. While he worked, his mind returned again and again to Luke's plan to become a high school teacher. Before classes began, he went to see his advisor and discovered that with a minimum of time and trouble, he could change his major from Agriculture to Vocational-Agriculture and add a teaching option. His advisor told him that even if he never went into the classroom full-time, he would be qualified as a substitute teacher.

Both Drew and Liz took extra fall and winter classes and time flew by for them. One evening in late November, as they sat in the living room reading their separate textbooks, Liz let out a little gasp and her hand went to her abdomen. She did not immediately answer when Drew asked if she was okay, but sat there with a look of wonder on her face.

"Lizzie?" Drew asked insistently. "What's wrong?"

"I've been so busy I didn't pay attention, but…" her voice trailed off as she thought back over the past couple of months, and then she smiled at Drew. "I think I need to go see Anna!"

"Anna?" Drew asked looking confused.

"Yes, Anna, the midwife, because she delivers babies, you know, and I think I just might be pregnant."

"Really?" Drew grinned, but then he sobered almost immediately. "But you haven't had morning sickness or anything, have you?" Drew asked. "How do you know you're pregnant?"

"I didn't have morning sickness with Belle either," she said. "I'll have to check my calendar, but I think my last cycle was just after Trish's wedding."

"Don't you think you should see a doctor?" Drew asked worriedly.

"I feel completely comfortable with Anna. She knows what she's doing, and she'd be the first to send me to a doctor or the hospital if I need to go," Liz assured him.

For the next few months, sewing for Liz and a new baby was added to the list of things to do. In sharp contrast to the first time, Liz breezed through this pregnancy on a wave of happiness and anticipation. Anna delivered little Mazelle Jean in the middle of the night on April 12th, and everyone immediately began calling her Mazie. With Grandma Mazelle watching her namesake during the day, Liz finished her course of study and graduated in May, thankful for the summer sessions she'd attended, which allowed her to graduate ahead of schedule.

Drew doted on his daughter, and Liz took to mothering as if she'd had a dozen children already. When Mazie was almost two, Liz discovered that she was pregnant again and went to see Anna. During one of her checkups, Anna got a funny look on her face and moved the stethoscope to another spot on Liz's abdomen listening intently. She moved the stethoscope and listened again. When she had done that several times, Liz asked anxiously, "What's wrong, Anna?"

"Oh, sorry!" Anna smiled. "This is only the second time this has happened to me, so I wanted to be sure."

"Excuse me?" Liz asked in confusion. "Second time what's happened to you?"

"Twins, dear." Anna beamed at her. "I just heard two heartbeats. You are expecting two babies this time." Liz walked home from Anna's house without noticing any of the scenery along the way.

"Twins?" Drew repeated when Liz gave him the news that evening. "Two babies?"

"Yeah," Liz said, shaking her head. "I haven't quite gotten used to the idea either."

"Did Anna want you to see a doctor?" Drew asked.

"No," Liz laughed. "And I'm not sure what good it would do. One of my classmates saw an obstetrician for her whole pregnancy, and he never figured out she was having twins. Not only that, but he thought she called him too early in her labor, so he took his time getting to the hospital, and by the time he showed up, the nurses had already delivered both babies."

"I'll bet she still had to pay his full fee, though, huh?"

"Of course," Liz replied. "I'll stick with Anna until she tells me I need a hospital."

Drew and Liz both went around in a daze for the next few weeks, not only about expecting twins, but also because the babies were due at the same time Drew was set to graduate.

He felt a little overwhelmed. While he prepared for graduation and was responsible for an expectant wife, a daughter and Grandma Mazelle, he was also pre-occupied with the problem of where to work. The plans he'd made when he and Lizzie got married - to go to school and then move back to his family's farm - didn't seem to fit him anymore. A lot of things had changed in the past few years.

Drew thought maybe he was pre-disposed to a three-generation household, having grown up with his Grandpa Joe living on the farm in close enough proximity to share the supper table most nights. In any case, no matter how healthy Mazelle seemed to be, she was seventy-five now, and he didn't think she should live alone, not that he would dare tell her that. He couldn't imagine leaving her in Havre and he knew she wouldn't want to move to Shelby. Grandma Mazelle's needs aside, he was pretty sure Lizzie didn't want to move, and neither did he.

He was still mulling over the problem in early March when Mazelle's son James came to visit. Drew assumed James had come to see his mother about business since James handled all the details of leasing Mazelle's farm. After a supper of fried chicken and potato salad, they were just finishing their coffee and apple pie when James cleared his throat and said he had something he'd like to discuss with Drew and Liz. Surprised, they sat up and prepared to listen.

He explained that the man to whom Mazelle's farm land was leased had developed some health problems and he would be unable to finish out the terms of the lease. It was late to make a change since it would soon be time to seed, and that put them in a bit of a bad spot.

"I'm here to see if you might be interested in taking on the lease," James said. Drew was taken completely by surprise and didn't answer right away. With a glance at Mazelle, James explained that he and his brother and sister had already discussed asking Drew if he was interested in buying the farm, but planned to wait until the lease was up at the end of the season. It was obvious from her lack of surprise that Mazelle had been aware of everything her children had been discussing. James had finished with a smile at his mother and the comment, "Pete and Caroline and I don't worry so much about Mom with you two living here." Mazelle had raised her eyebrows at him over that remark, but Drew could tell she appreciated his concern. He also suspected he knew where the idea to approach him had come from.

Drew glanced across the table at Liz, she nodded, and with not a word of discussion, they accepted the proposal on the spot. Drew told James he was definitely interested in purchasing the farm, but said he thought they should wait to discuss that after he finished the current lease. That would give them time to get comfortable with him on a business level. Privately, he also thought it would give him a chance to figure out how to approach his dad about the whole idea. That was the tough part. Drew and his dad had always talked about him taking over the farm one day, and he had honestly looked at his years in college as a postponement of that agreement. He didn't want his dad to think he was rejecting his legacy or anything, it was just that Havre had become home to him and to Lizzie. He wracked his brain to think of a way to explain that yes, he wanted to farm, but he wanted to take over someone else's farm instead of theirs, and to explain it without hurting his dad's feelings.

The twins arrived two weeks before graduation on May 16th, and were named Wyatt Phillip and Joseph Andrew. Both sets of parents and Grandpa Joe came to see Drew receive his diploma, to meet their new grandsons, and to spoil Mazie, who was utterly thrilled with her role as big sister.

Liz's parents left the day after graduation, since Liz's brother John was graduating from high school the following week. Drew knew the time had come for him to have a talk with his dad, so the next morning he invited him to come and see the acreage. They walked to the barn and got into the old pickup and set off, talking about acreage and crops. Drew explained how James had asked him to take over the farm when the lease was dropped at the last minute, and that he'd accepted.

"James said if Lizzie and I want to stay here, we can buy the farm. What do you think, Dad?"

"It's a nice place, son," John replied. "I think you could make a good living here."

"I feel bad, though. I always thought I'd come back home, but…" his voice trailed off.

"But now this has become home?" John asked, with a knowing twinkle in his eye.

"I guess so, yeah," Drew admitted. "We always talked about me taking over our farm though, and I wouldn't be able to do both."

"That's true," John said with a smile. Drew thought that his dad seemed to be taking this news better than he'd expected, and then as John began to explain, he understood.

"Grandpa Joe decided to get an apartment in town, so Luke and Trish moved into his place on the farm." Drew knew that and nodded.

"Luke hasn't said anything to me yet. I don't think he wants to butt in between you and me, but Trish told your mom that they would love to buy our place."

"Really? I thought Luke was focused on teaching," Drew said in surprise.

"According to what Trish has told mom, he thinks he can do both," John explained. "His idea is that he can teach while he helps me. That way, I can keep farming while I teach him the rest of what he needs to know to run the place. And I don't have to retire until I'm ready."

"You know, that might just work."

"And the farm would stay in the family," John added. "So it works out for everybody." Drew nodded in agreement. Thinking about it later, Drew concluded that Luke and John probably worked together better than Drew and his dad did. He chuckled thinking how Grandma Mazelle always said things usually had a way of working out. She also said that honesty was the best policy, and he was glad he'd been honest with his father.

When he told Mazelle about all the worrying he and Luke and his dad had done over the farm issue, she smiled and said he should learn from the experience and cultivate a habit of addressing issues and solving problems as they came up, instead of letting them fester in his mind like a sliver. He had cause to remember that advice several times as the years passed.

XIV

Mazie, Wyatt & Joey

Ten Years Later

Drew had a lot of time to think while he worked on equipment, and this week he was getting the equipment ready for seeding. He wiped his greasy hands on a rag and put away his tools as he reminisced.

It was hard to believe the years had passed so quickly. Mazie was fourteen now, and the twins were nearly twelve. Liz started teaching third grade when the boys started first grade, and she loved her work. Grandma Mazelle had slowed down a little, but at eighty-five she still walked a mile or two every day, puttered in the garden, and kept up with her church and social activities. The farm kept him busy enough. He still thought about teaching high school, but there were no openings in his field at the moment, so he did a little substitute teaching and enjoyed his lifestyle. All in all, he thought, as he headed toward the house, life was good. As he walked by the barn on his way to the house, Mazie called to him from the door of the bunkhouse.

"Dad, we need to talk to you." She motioned for him to come inside. Curious as to what was going on, and knowing from experience that when Mazie was involved, there was definitely something going on, Drew entered the bunkhouse and looked around. The place was a lot bigger than it had been when he first saw it after the war. During his senior year in college, when one of his instructors had been looking for a construction project where the students could gain practical experience, Drew consulted with Mazelle and then presented a plan for enlarging the bunkhouse. Mazelle paid for the building materials, and the ten Vo-Ag students did the work, practicing basic carpentry skills they had studied as part of their course work. They contacted an electrician and a plumber to help with the project, but both of them donated their labor and charged only for their supplies. The instructor was pleased and not all that surprised. Drew had been puzzled until Mazelle explained what she called the human side of their local economy. It turned out that the electrician had a daughter who was to be married that summer, and he wondered if some of their guests could use the bunkhouse. Mazelle readily agreed. The plumber, overhearing the exchange, mentioned that his church was hosting a revival whose members would need housing for a week in September. Drew was familiar with farmers helping other farmers in case of injury or machinery problems, and was glad that the same policy of neighbors helping neighbors was alive and well in Havre.

The roof was extended and two large rooms were added to the side of the barn, each with a large window. In the new room to the right of the main entrance, bunk beds were built in on each side of the window with trundle beds underneath them. The space under the window was occupied by a large chest for storage of the bedding. Two more sets of bunks lined the opposite wall, so there were ten beds in all. The room on the other side of the hallway was large enough to hold two beds, and at the end of the hall, in the original bunkhouse room there was another bed. Originally that room had been big enough for two beds, but the room was a little smaller now because the bathroom next door had been enlarged enough to include a shower and some cabinets for towels.

Mazie stood with her arms folded beside one of the windows, silhouetted by the afternoon sunlight and looking very serious indeed. She was nearly as tall as her mother, with the same blonde hair and brown eyes. Wyatt and Joey sat side by side on one of the bunks and as much as Mazie looked like her mother, the boys resembled him, tall for their age, with dark brown hair and gray eyes. Right now both pairs of gray eyes were fixed on him, and they looked quite serious, too.

"What's this about? Is something wrong?" Drew asked, worried now.

It was Mazie who answered. "It's about Mom."

"What about her?" Drew asked.

"Well, she gets depressed every year in the winter."

"Yeah, Dad, we saw her crying last week," Joey chimed in.

"She cried last year too, Dad," Mazie said. "I remember because you brought her flowers the week after Valentine's Day."

"I see," Drew said. "So you think she cried because I brought her flowers?"

"No, Dad! I thought you brought her flowers because she was depressed." Mazie rolled her eyes impatiently. "At first I thought she was upset because you didn't bring her flowers for Valentine's Day, but then I remembered you brought her chocolates."

"You are observant, aren't you?" Drew said in amazement.

"Kids notice things, Dad," Mazie replied seriously. "Like you always bring her chocolates for Valentine's Day and then you bring her pink flowers the next week."

"Have you mentioned this to Mom?" Drew asked.

"Um, no," Mazie replied.

"That's your job," Wyatt informed him, and Joey nodded in agreement.

Either Mazie had given them instructions about this interview, and they were following them, or they agreed with her analysis of the situation. Drew knew that when his three offspring agreed on something, they were a force to be reckoned with. The last time they had agreed on something, the family had suddenly acquired a dog named Wilbur.

"My job? You want me to find out why your mom is depressed?" Drew asked. All three children nodded.

Drew ran his fingers through his hair while his mind scrambled. He knew exactly why Lizzie got depressed in February every year, but he wasn't sure his children were ready to hear that story. He needed to discuss this with Lizzie.

"I'll talk to her about it."

"Okay. Thanks, Dad." Mazie hugged him and the three kids filed out of the bunkhouse and went back to the house. Later that evening Drew told Lizzie what the children had decided about her February bout of the blues.

"I'm sorry, Drew, I really try not to let Belle's birthday get to me every year, but, well, I guess I'm not doing a very good job if the kids have noticed." Liz shook her head, clearly upset.

"Do you think we should just tell them?" Drew asked.

"Maybe," Lizzie said slowly. "I always planned to tell them at some point; it's just hard to know when they are ready to hear it. Since they've noticed, oh, I don't know. It will be a difficult conversation. Let's think about it for a day or two, okay?"

Anna sat in Mazelle's kitchen with a cup of coffee and a rhubarb muffin. "I never think to use rhubarb in muffins. I usually make pie or cobbler with it. These are wonderful." She shook her head and looked down at the table. "But of course I didn't stop by to chat about muffins."

"What's wrong, Anna?" Mazelle asked.

Anna closed her eyes for a moment and took a deep breath. "Belle's mom passed away last month. That's why I made a trip down to Wyoming -- for the funeral."

"Oh, Anna! I'm so sorry!" Mazelle exclaimed.

"Her health was never good, which probably contributed to all the miscarriages, or maybe the miscarriages are why she was always a little frail. It's hard to say, but nobody expected… well, anyway, it was sudden, a stroke." Anna paused and wiped her eyes. Mazelle reached over and placed a comforting hand on her arm. Anna steadied her voice and went on. "Her name was Debbie, she was only forty-three, and she was the sweetest person. Matt is devastated, and so is Belle. The whole family is in shock, me included. Forty-three, Mazelle!"

"I'm so sorry, for you and your family, and especially for Belle and her dad."

"Thank you. Matt is a doctor like his dad and grandfather. He thinks he somehow should have known and been able to treat Debbie. That's his grief talking, of course, not his medical training. Anyway, I'm rambling." Anna took a sip of her coffee and a couple of deep breaths before she continued. "Belle looks a lot like Liz and Mazie. Enough so that if you met her on the street you would know that she was related. When I was there for the funeral, I spent quite a bit of time with her, because, well, she needed to talk to someone and I was there and willing."

"Of course she sought you out. You have an aura that invites people to confide in you. It's one of the things that makes you so good with people." Mazelle nodded in understanding.

"Yes, well, now she wants to come and spend the summer with me," Anna burst out.

"Oh my goodness!" Mazelle exclaimed, her eyes widening.

"You see why I'm in a tizzy? Matt has been planning a medical mission trip to India or somewhere with a group of other doctors. He's one of the organizers, and they've been planning this for nearly a year, so he doesn't want to back out and leave the rest of the team in the lurch."

"He is in a tough spot, isn't he?" Mazelle sympathized. "I remember when Robby died unexpectedly. It seemed like it upset everything in my life. One has to adapt to the suddenness as well as the loss."

"I think that's what is going on with Matt. He and Debbie had this all worked out, and now he doesn't know how to adapt the plan. The main thing that changes is that Belle can't stay alone, of course."

"No, of course she can't, even if she was old enough, which she isn't quite, she shouldn't be alone right after losing her mother," Mazelle agreed.

"So Matt is considering staying home and trying to find someone to go in his place."

"And I suppose that will be difficult at this late date."

"Belle doesn't want him to stay home because of her. She's been in on the plan all along and thinks it is a good thing her dad is doing. And she doesn't want to stay with Matt's sister and her husband, because they are retired and there would be nothing for her to do. I told her there isn't much to do here, either, and I offered to come and stay at their house instead, but she insisted that she needs to get away."

"That poor girl!" Mazelle exclaimed.

"My heart goes out to her, and I'd dearly love to have her, but, well, you can see how that would be a problem." Anna was more upset than Mazelle had ever seen her.

"Anna, it's not the end of the world, and let's be honest, Belle is old enough to know about her own history." She sipped her coffee thinking. "Did her parents tell her about the adoption?"

"I'm not sure. I don't really think so, but I can check."

"Depending on that, and her reaction, we'll know where to go from there." Mazelle was thinking through the problem out loud.

"I assumed she'd be curious about and want to meet Liz, but she might hate the idea, is that what you're saying?" Anna asked.

"Liz was eighteen when she had Belle, and I remember she said that she'd been trying to put herself in Belle's place and see how she'd feel if she found out she was adopted. She was convinced she'd want to know the circumstances of her birth. That rang true to me, but that would be under normal circumstances, wouldn't you think?"

"Normal meaning she hadn't just suddenly lost her mother," Anna stated, nodding. "Yes, I see what you mean. We don't know how she'll react under these circumstances. You're right. Matt needs to tell her so she has time to think about things before he leaves, and she can ask him whatever questions she has."

"That's what I think," Mazelle agreed.

"She could decide not to come here after all," Anna mused.

"Possibly. And if she does, that's the end of it, at least for now. But if she still wants to come, then we have to think about how to let her know that her, I hate to use the term "real mother" because Debbie was her real mother. I'm not sure what to call Liz."

"Biological mother," Anna supplied automatically.

"Yes, thank you. We'll have to think about how to let her know that her biological mother is your neighbor."

"It would be a lot easier if I just told her she couldn't come here, and I went there instead," Anna said doubtfully.

"Oh, it might be easier in the short-term. But the easy way is not usually the right way, as you and I have discussed on many occasions."

"I know." Anna sighed, remembering when her own mother died. She sat there for a few moments in silence. "I was twelve when my mom died, and I remember how awful that time was for me and for my dad. I suppose if I'd had a chance to go somewhere else for awhile, I would have done exactly that."

"She did say, straight out, that she needs a break. Maybe she instinctively knows what would be best for her right now. Maybe she also needs her Aunt Anna. She does seem to have forged a connection with you, and she is missing her mother," Mazelle said.

"Who knew trying to find the best home for a baby would lead to this?" Anna asked ruefully.

"Life has some strange twists and turns, that's for sure," Mazelle agreed. "I don't think finding out about the adoption will change Belle's mind about coming here, but if it does, I think she will still want to come someday, so that means Matt isn't the only one with things to explain. Drew and Liz have some things to talk to their children about, too," Mazelle said.

"Thank you, Mazelle. You are a good friend." Anna blinked back tears. "I really needed to discuss this."

"You're welcome, dear, but keep in mind Belle is my great-grandchild and I have always hoped I'd get to see her before I die. I could have ulterior motives all over the place."

"Are you planning to die anytime soon?" Anna asked dryly, as she prepared to leave.

"Well no, but at my age, one must be prepared," Mazelle reminded her with a smile as Anna stepped off the porch.

She was such a fraud, Mazelle thought to herself, acting all calm and reasonable when her insides were wriggling like a pail of snakes. She didn't feel like she had one wise thought in her head. Oh, her words were true enough; she did believe in telling the truth and in addressing problems and dealing with them, but she didn't think it was going to be near as easy as she just made it sound. Later that evening, when Mazelle was sure the children were down for the night, she found Drew and Liz in the living room.

"I have a fresh pot of tea in the kitchen, and something to tell the two of you." Liz looked up in concern, glanced at Drew, who shook his head to indicate he didn't know what was going on. The two of them followed Mazelle to the kitchen. Mazelle took a seat at the table, waited for them to pour themselves cups of tea and sit down.

"I have a story to tell you." She said seriously.

"Okay, we're listening," Liz said. Mazelle explained how Anna's nephew and his wife ended up being Belle's adopted parents.

"And you knew this?" Liz asked in surprise.

"I suspected. I never asked Anna, and Anna didn't say anything to me either. Until today. Everything changed today."

"What happened today?" Liz asked. Mazelle took a fortifying sip of tea and continued her story, beginning with the sad news that Belle's mother had died shortly after Belle's seventeenth birthday, and ending with how Belle wanted to spend the summer with her Aunt Anna. When she finished, Liz sat unmoving and silent for over a minute. Drew stood up and paced the length of the kitchen and back.

"I never expected to see her," Drew said, stopping in front of the table. "I know the two of you have always hoped that you'd see her one day, but I honestly thought it was such a remote possibility that I put it out of my mind."

"Belle," Liz whispered. "We'll be able to see Belle."

"We need to focus on what effect this will have on Mazie, Wyatt and Joey. We have to decide what to tell them and when." Drew said. "Right, Lizzie?"

Liz's eyes filled with tears. "I know. We've already talked about whether or not to tell them, now we have no choice. But I'm not looking forward to it. I'm not sure what they'll think of me for getting pregnant so young."

"*You* didn't get pregnant, *we* got pregnant. It always takes two, you know. Our kids need to know that, especially the twins. If we say we believe in telling the truth, then we need to tell the truth," Drew said firmly.

"Okay," Liz said reluctantly. "When?"

"I think the sooner the better. How about this weekend?" Drew said.

XV

Explanations

"Belle, honey," Matt said nervously. "I need to talk to you about something."

His daughter was beautiful with shoulder length blonde hair, an oval face and brown eyes, but she had lost her sparkle when her mom died. Lately, he often found her the way she was today, sitting at the kitchen table staring into space, her chin cupped in her hand. It made his heart ache to see her so sad and listless. Since Debbie died, he felt the same way though, like a hole had been ripped in his life, and he didn't know what to do about it except get up every day and keep breathing.

"Is it about your trip?" she asked, without much interest.

"No." He had no idea how to do this, but Anna had called him instead of writing. She said she didn't want a letter lying around where Belle might find it. She told him all the pieces of the adoption story that he hadn't known and she stressed how important it was for him to have this conversation with Belle, and soon.

Matt remembered how happy they had been when Belle had come into their lives. He and Debbie had promised they would tell Belle about her biological mother, and he felt a flash of irritation, not with Debbie, but because she had died before Belle's eighteenth birthday. Now he had to do the telling without Debbie's help and didn't know how to go about it.

"Dad?" Belle prompted him. "What do you need to talk to me about?" Matt snapped out of his reverie, laid a folder on the table and sat down across from his daughter. Folding his hands on top of the folder, he took a deep breath, looked her square in the eye.

"Your mother and I couldn't have children."

"What?" Belle asked, dumbfounded. She shook her head. "I know where babies come from Dad, so don't try to say the stork brought me!"

"No, of course not." Matt rubbed his face with both hands. "I'm sorry. That was a dumb way to start. Damn! I'm no good at this."

"Just tell me, Dad," Belle said. "If you couldn't have kids and the stork didn't bring me," she paused and then her eyes widened in shock, "I'm adopted?"

"Yes. Yes, you are." Matt was relieved to have the first hurdle behind him. "We adopted you right after you were born."

Belle couldn't think of a single thing to say. She sat staring at the man she'd called *Dad* for her whole life. It had never occurred to her that she wasn't his natural daughter. She thought back, adding up the similarities. Matt had brown eyes and blond hair, like she did. Her mother's hair had also been blonde, but with a natural curl, and she'd had hazel eyes. Of course there were differences, too. Her mom had been short, just over five feet tall. Her dad was five feet ten, or so. But she was five feet six, so that was reasonable. Her mom had a heart-shaped face, her dad had a square jaw and her face was more oval. She had noticed these details without giving them much thought, but now they seemed to take on new importance. Belle glared at her dad.

"Why didn't you and Mom ever tell me?" she demanded.

"We planned to tell you, but we never seemed to find the right time."

"What do you mean by the right time?"

"Well, we kept setting deadlines at ages when you would be old enough to know, but then we chickened out," Matt admitted.

"What ages?" Belle demanded.

"Eight was too young, twelve was right at puberty and sixteen, well, obviously, we didn't do it then either."

"That's pathetic, Dad," Belle said rolling her eyes.

"Yeah, I guess it was. I think maybe we just didn't want to admit that you weren't ours, biologically speaking," Matt said with a sigh. "Let me start at the beginning."

"That would be a great idea." Belle snapped, angrily. Her fists clenched on the table in front of her. Matt sat quietly for a minute, gathering his thoughts, and then he told her how he and Debbie had come to adopt her. But Belle's irritation fell away as she listened without interruption, periodically wiping her eyes with a tissue. Matt explained how Debbie had finally pulled herself together after a year of depression and listlessness, signed up for nurse's training, and decided to focus on working with him in his practice.

"But she wasn't happy, and I couldn't stand it." Matt said desperately. "I loved her so much and I couldn't stand her being sad, deep down to her soul. She held it together during the day, but she cried in her sleep."

"So how did you get me?" Belle asked.

"I knew my Aunt Anna was a midwife in Montana."

"Aunt Anna?" Belle repeated.

"Yes. I wrote to her and explained our situation and asked if she could help us adopt a child. She wrote back to us and said she had a patient, an eighteen-year-old girl, who was going to have to give her baby up for adoption." Matt stopped again, remembering the look on Debbie's face when they got that letter.

"And?" Belle prompted.

Matt's attention snapped back to the present and he continued. "Anna told us to be ready to come sometime in February, so we packed a suitcase and waited. You were in your mom's arms within an hour or so after you were born."

"Mom told me I was named after Aunt Anna, because her name is Annabelle."

"You were, but we weren't the ones who decided that." Matt opened the folder he had set on the table and extracted a single sheet of paper. Handing it across the table, he said, "This is the letter your biological mother wrote to us. It was in the box of baby things, right on top." He waited while she scanned the lines on the paper. Her eyes widened when she finished.

"Her name was Elizabeth," Belle said, looking up at him. "My middle name."

"Yes." Matt reached into the folder again and handed her another piece of paper. "This is a copy of the letter we wrote to Anna just before your first birthday. We asked Anna to let her know you were okay." Once again he waited.

"Wow." Belle breathed. "You and mom kept the name she'd given me and then named me after her, too."

"Well, we both thought she was a very brave young woman, and without her sacrifice, we wouldn't have had you."

"What else is in the folder?"

"As I mentioned, when Anna delivered you to us, she also brought a box of baby things. They were all hand sewn, little gowns and…"

"I've seen those things. Mom kept them in her trunk," Belle interrupted.

"She kept them to show you that Liz, that's what Anna calls her – Liz – did everything she could for you. Knowing she couldn't keep you, she still made clothes and blankets, and…" He opened the folder for a third time and extracted three sheets of pink stationary covered in neat handwriting. "This was tucked into the bottom of the box, folded inside a knitted baby blanket." He handed them to Belle, and while she read, he got up and poured two glasses of iced tea. He brought them to the table and sat quietly sipping his until Belle had finished reading. She looked at him with tears in her eyes.

"This is like a diary of her pregnancy," she choked out.

"I know. You were greatly loved by both of your mothers, Belle."

"I'm glad you finally told me, Dad."

"Me, too." Matt answered, but his smile didn't quite reach his eyes. He had told Belle about her adoption, but telling her the rest of the story would have to wait for another day, because he couldn't deal with it right now. And that day that would have to come pretty soon because he had just three weeks before he left for India.

"Kids," Drew said as they finished with supper Friday evening. "Your mother and I want to talk to you about something."

All three of his children looked at him warily, each wondering if they'd done something to warrant a family meeting. None of them spoke, and neither did Liz or Drew. The silence stretched until finally, Mazie said impatiently, "Well? What is it?"

"You know that I was in the army during the war, right?" Drew began. Three heads nodded. "Well, did you know that your mom and I went together during high school?"

"Grandma Jean told me that," Mazie said, while the boys looked on in bewilderment.

"Okay." Drew ran his fingers through his hair and looked at Liz, but she was staring fixedly at the table. No help there, he decided, and it wasn't fair to appeal to Mazelle. It was very tempting, but it wasn't fair, so he took a breath and began again. "Well, your mom and I loved each other very much. We were planning to get married when she graduated from high school. I'd already bought the ring and everything, but then I got my orders to go off to fight in a war." He paused, looking at each of his children before continuing. "And I was very, very afraid."

"What were you afraid of, Dad?" Joey asked. He could not believe that his dad had ever been afraid of anything.

"I was afraid I might be badly injured, or even killed. I was afraid that Lizzie and I might never see each other again. So I did a very dumb thing."

"What?" Wyatt asked. First scared and now dumb. They were learning things about their dad that he, personally, wasn't sure he wanted to know.

"Well," Drew shook his head in disgust. "I told your mom that I might not come back and she should just find a new boyfriend."

"Dad!" Mazie exclaimed. "That was dumb with a capital D."

"Yes, well, I figured that out within a few days, but by then I was in the army and I couldn't talk to your mom and explain that I didn't mean it."

"I don't think I want to know this," Mazie said. "Everything turned out okay, so…"

"Stay with me on this, Mazie, because you do need to know. Trust me, you all need to know," Drew assured her, and when he was sure he had their attention, he went on. "So guess what your mom did?"

"She cried?" Joey asked, with a glance at his mother.

"Yes, she did," Drew smiled sadly. "And it was my fault."

"It wasn't your fault." Liz interrupted unexpectedly. All eyes turned to her and she continued, looking at each of her three children in turn. "When your dad found out he had to leave, we stopped discussing important things. If we'd been honest with each other, things would have been different."

"What do you mean, Mom?" Mazie asked.

"I mean that instead of talking to each other, your dad tried to protect me, and I cried."

"Girls cry sometimes," Wyatt said looking between his father and his mother, "That's okay, right?"

"There isn't anything wrong with crying," Liz said with a smile. "Crying helps us get over being hurt or sad. But crying doesn't solve anything."

"Your mom had a reason for crying, besides me being dumb with a capital D. You see, after I went off to war, your mom realized that she was going to have a baby."

Dead silence greeted this statement. Three pairs of eyes stared at him, stared at Liz, and stared at him again.

"Then what happened?" Mazie demanded. "Because I know you were married before I was born. I checked."

"You did?" Liz asked, looking up in surprise.

"Me and my friends, well, we all know if our parents were married long enough when we were born, Mom. It's not that hard to figure out."

"Oh?" Liz asked curiously. "How do you figure it out?"

"By looking at the dates on family pictures or asking which anniversary it is. I found your wedding date in Grandma's Bible. Once you have the dates, it's simple math." Mazie shrugged.

"Do you guys know this stuff, too?" Liz asked the boys. They nodded, not in the least embarrassed by the subject matter.

"It's easy," Joey said. "And anyway, it doesn't matter to us." Liz and Drew exchanged a glance.

"Interesting," Drew muttered. "So where was I?"

"You were telling us mom was going to have a baby," Mazie reminded him. "And I want to know what happened to that baby!"

"Okay, I'm getting there. Don't want to skip anything. Your mom came here to live with Grandma Mazelle, and she had the baby, and, well, she gave the baby for adoption," Drew explained, relieved to have finally said the words.

"Oh, good," Mazie said with a relieved sigh.

"Good?" Liz asked, surprised and curious at her reaction.

"Yeah, I was afraid the baby died or something," Mazie explained. "That'd be so sad!"

Liz looked at her daughter in amazement. "You're right. I guess I was focused on the wrong thing. I thought it was horribly sad to give my baby up for adoption, which it was, but I should have been grateful I had a healthy child."

"So do we have a sister or a brother out there somewhere?" Wyatt wanted to know.

"A sister," Liz replied. "Her name is Belle Elizabeth, and she had her seventeenth birthday on February 22nd of this year."

"Oh!" Mazie exclaimed, "So, is that why you get sad every winter?"

Liz nodded. "Yes, I always remember her birthday, and it makes me sad for a few days."

"Well, that clears that up," Mazie said, and immediately asked how the baby came to be named Belle Elizabeth. Liz explained the chain of events that led to the name, how Anna delivered the baby, and when she had finished, Joey asked if that was all.

"Actually, there is a little more to the story," Drew said, and he explained that Anna was the midwife who delivered Belle.

"Dad!" Wyatt said impatiently. "Mom just said that when she told us about the name."

"But what I'm getting at is that Anna is *related* to Belle." He stopped and looked at Mazelle, who hadn't said a single word throughout the entire discussion.

"Would you mind taking it from here?" he asked. "I could use a break." She smiled at him, and when she had the attention of all three children, continued the story, telling them what she had learned from Anna earlier that week.

"Belle wants to come here? And stay with Anna?" Mazie asked in excitement. "We'll be able to meet her? That would be neat! I've always wanted a sister!"

"If she comes and if she *wants* to meet us, then, yes." Drew said. "We have to wait and see about all the 'ifs'."

"So, can we be excused now?" Joey asked again. Drew nodded, and the boys headed out the door. Mazie stood up more slowly and went to hug her mother.

"I hope Belle comes, Mom, and I hope she wants to meet us."

"Me too, sweetie, me too." Liz whispered in a shaky voice.

Matt tossed and turned, unable to sleep, and finally decided to get up and fix himself a cup of that tea Anna had given him when she came for Debbie's funeral. Chamomile, he thought it was, and she had said it might help him sleep. Throwing back the covers, he slid his feet into slippers and grabbed his robe, belting it around his waist as he made his way toward the kitchen. The light was already on, and Belle sat at the table with a cup of tea in front of her. She was focused on the items from the folder he'd given her last week.

"Dad!" she said startled.

"Couldn't sleep. And you couldn't either, I see." Belle shook her head. "Something bothering you?"

"I think there has to be more to the story," she replied. "My story, I mean, about the adoption and all."

"There is," Matt agreed. He fixed himself a cup of tea and sat down. "You read the entries on the pink sheets, the ones that told about Liz's boyfriend going off to war?" Belle nodded.

"After you were born and we adopted you, Liz had a hard time. Anna didn't tell us much, but enough for us to know that she felt really bad about losing you. She finally pulled herself together and decided to stay with her grandma and go to college in Havre. When the war ended, her boyfriend came looking for her, because he never stopped loving her. He had no idea about you, so they had to work through that, which took awhile. Anyway, when they got everything settled between them, they got married."

"Did they live happily ever after?" Belle asked hopefully.

"Well, they've stayed together, so I guess they have. I never met either of them, so all I have to go on is what Anna has recently told me."

"Recently?" Belle asked, sitting up a little straighter in her chair.

"Oh, yes. Anna knew your mom and I had promised to tell you all these things, and she was not happy to hear that we hadn't done it. She called me and said I needed to tell you right away, and then she gave me a list of things you needed to know so I wouldn't forget anything."

"Why is it suddenly so important after all this time? Is it because Mom died?"

"I suppose that had something to do with it, because if Mom hadn't died you wouldn't want to go and spend the summer with Anna."

"What does spending the summer with Anna have to do with anything?" Belle cocked her head and waited for his reply.

"Anna didn't want you to arrive at her house without all the background information you needed to deal with the situation you'll find there."

"What situation?" Belle asked suspiciously.

"Liz and her husband Drew, that's your other dad's name, live next door to her."

"They do?" Belle asked in a strangled voice. Matt nodded. "So I will probably meet them this summer?"

"Yes. Well, if you spend the summer at Anna's house, you will." Matt answered, nodding again.

"Do you know anything about them?"

"Anna told me that they have three children, a girl and twin boys." Matt waited for more questions.

"Do they know about me?"

"They probably do by now," Matt said with a shrug. "When you said you wanted to go to Anna's, it set everything in motion. I hadn't told you about the adoption and Liz and Drew hadn't told their children, either, according to what I heard. I guess we were all going to do it 'someday', and well…"

"Someday is here," Belle said.

"Exactly. None of us knew how you'd take this news, but you seem okay with it. And I've told you all I know, but as Liz wrote in her letter, you're free to ask her questions when you meet her, if you like."

"Is it okay with you if I meet her?"

"I'd like for you to meet her. I think she must be a special lady since she gave me and your mom the greatest gift in the world…you."

"Thanks, Dad." She got up to hug him, and then added, "Oh wait, I do have one more question. Are there other relatives?"

"Your great-grandma Mazelle is in her eighties and lives with Drew and Liz and their children, next door to Anna. Beyond that, I don't know. You can ask Anna, or wait until you get there and ask Liz."

"Okay. Good night, Dad." Belle said absently.

Matt, with a lighter heart and a clear conscience, went back to bed and slept like a baby for the first time since his wife had died.

Belle was thoughtful as she returned to her room and climbed into bed. She lay there for a long time, staring into the darkness and thinking about this other family she'd recently learned about. Her dad said he wanted her to meet them and she decided her mother probably would want her to get to know them, too. It was going to be a very interesting summer.

XVI

Belle Returns

It was Wednesday afternoon during the first week of June when Matt and Belle pulled into Anna's driveway. They'd taken two days to make the six hundred and seventy mile trip from Laramie, driving to Billings the first day, and from Billings to Havre the next. Although tired from two days in the car, Belle looked eagerly out the window curious to see what Anna's house looked like. What she saw was a sprawling stone cottage with a chimney on one end. There was a garden off to one side, an apple tree in the front yard, a variety of other trees scattered around the property, and flowers tumbling from assorted baskets and pots lining the path to the back door. An old bike leaned against the porch, which spanned the width of the structure. The porch was littered with chairs, a table, and more pots of flowers. She knew two things right away. The porch looked like an inviting place to relax, and Anna definitely had a green thumb!

The weary travelers stepped out of their car just as a teenage girl emerged from the door, carrying three cartons of eggs. The girl stopped dead in her tracks and stared at Belle, while Belle froze beside the car and stared back.

Mazie recovered first, She hopped off the porch and moved toward the car. "You must be Belle! Oh my gosh! You look just like Mom. I'm Mazie, we're sisters, you know? I've been dying to meet you! I hope you like us, our family, I mean." She stopped talking suddenly and looked embarrassed.

Anna had emerged from the house a few steps behind Mazie and held her breath as she watched the two girls meet for the first time and listened to Mazie's comments.

"Yeah, I'm Belle. It's nice to meet you, Mazie." Belle replied. Looking at Mazie was almost like looking into a mirror. It startled her that they looked so much alike.

"I've got to get home with the eggs. Grandma is making a cake," Mazie said. "Wait til I tell them I got to see you first!" She sidled over to the bike, placed the eggs in the basket, and off she went, her legs pumping furiously as she peddled down the driveway.

"Well," Anna smiled as she stepped off the porch to welcome Belle and Matt with hugs. "If you had planned to slip in without being noticed, you'd better go to plan B."

Matt stood rooted to the spot, quite startled by the resemblance between Belle and Mazie. He raised his eyebrows at Anna. "Wow! Seems you forgot to tell us about the strong family resemblance. No doubt the two girls are sisters, is there?"

"I think I've spent so many years ignoring little things like that, I may have neglected to mention it. Sorry if you were taken by surprise. I'm sure you can understand why Belle needed to know about this before she came."

Matt nodded, still looking after Mazie. "Mazie didn't appear to be surprised."

"She's used to it, people comment on her resemblance to her mother all the time." Turning to Belle, Anna said, "How are you, dear?"

Belle had also been staring after Mazie and started at Anna's voice. "I'm fine, Aunt Anna. This is going to be a little strange."

"Everything new is a little strange, at least at first," Anna agreed. "Well, come in and have something cold to drink, before you unpack."

The door Mazie had just come out of led to Anna's kitchen with its white walls and honey-colored pine cupboards accented by a red-and-white checked tablecloth and chair cushions, and red towels and potholders. There was an herb garden in the windowsill above the sink, and a bright yellow vase of fresh daisies on the table. Anna walked to the refrigerator as she asked over her shoulder,

"Iced tea or lemonade?" Matt and Belle opted for iced tea and took seats at the table in the center of the room. Belle continued her perusal of the house. To the right of the door they'd just come through was an archway, beyond which she saw a laundry sink and a washing machine on one side of a narrow room, and cubicles, coat hooks with an assortment of jackets, sweaters and a raincoat hanging from them, and a bench with a pair of boots underneath it on the other side. In the opposite corner of the kitchen from that little room were two doorways, the one on the outside wall was closed, but the other one was open, revealing the corner of a dining table and chairs. Across from the entry was a wide hallway leading to the rest of the house.

When they had finished their iced tea, Matt went out to bring Belle's things in while Anna showed Belle the rest of the house and let her choose the bedroom she'd be using. There was a dining room on the left, as they walked down the hallway, the table and eight chairs in the center of the room, and a huge china cupboard taking up most of the back wall. A silver tea service sat on a silver tray on the china cupboard and there was a lace table runner with a vase of flowers on the table.

Across the hall from the dining room, the first door was closed, but a plaque on the door with the word *office* stenciled on it in italic letters explained its function. Next was a bathroom. It had white walls, white fixtures and cupboards, yellow towels and a yellow rug. There were sunflowers painted on the walls, a group of fairly large ones around the mirror over the sink, and smaller ones in a border around the top of the walls just below the ceiling. On the other side of the bathroom was Anna's bedroom. A quick glance revealed walls of pale eggshell. There were yellow-and-orange flowered curtains, a bright yellow bedspread strewn with pillows of all sizes in yellow, orange and red as well as some in the print that matched the curtains. Tall bookshelves stood on both sides of the window, and there was a bench under the window creating a window seat. It was covered with a bright orange cushion and strewn with more pillows.

"You like bright colors, don't you?" Belle commented. Anna laughed and said that bright cheerful colors made her happy.

The living room was straight ahead, with a stone fireplace, more bookshelves, an old upright piano, several comfortable looking chairs, a couch, and a smattering of small tables. They didn't enter the living room, but turned left into a hallway between the living room and dining room. Anna explained that there were three bedrooms and another bathroom at the end of this hall, and that Belle could choose which room she wanted for herself.

The first room on the left was a rather plain bathroom, with white walls and fixtures and blue curtains, rugs and towels. The bedroom across the hall looked like a man's room, with wood paneled walls, dark green curtains and a quilt in dark green and gold on the bed. The room beside the bathroom was painted pale green. It had curtains of white cotton with ruffled edges and a pale green chenille bedspread. The bed was piled with assorted pillows in pastel colors. The large window was framed on both sides with bookshelves. There was a bench under the window with a green cushion and more pastel pillows.

Belle knew she didn't have to look any further. She felt at home as soon as she stepped through the doorway. To be polite, she went across the hall and looked into the last bedroom. All the rooms had the same wood floors and pine furniture. Here the curtains and bedspread were a creamy lace and the walls a pale peach. There were low bookshelves under the windows and a rocking chair in the corner.

Belle turned to Anna just as Matt came down the hall with her two suitcases.

"It is a hard choice between the peaches and cream room and the green one, but I think I like the green room best," she said.

"I thought you might. I remember your room had a lot of pale green in it."

It didn't take long for Belle to unpack. As she put her things away she noticed two paintings on the wall above the bed. At first glance one was simply a meadow dotted with a vast assortment of wildflowers, and the other a forest scene with a doe and a fawn drinking from a stream that meandered along the edge of the trees. She was gazing absently at the one of the meadow, wondering who had painted them, when she saw the fairies in amongst the flowers. She made a more thorough inspection and found tiny little cottages under the wild rose bushes and clumps of daisies. Entranced, she turned her attention to the picture of the forest and soon located the fairies there, too, as well as their tiny houses nestled in the branches of the trees.

Belle walked across the hall and peeked into what she thought of as the peaches and cream room again. Here she found more paintings, this time a group of three, each depicting a white vase of flowers. The first picture was a pair of creamy white lilies with a butterfly on one petal. The white vase and the white lilies made the colors of the butterfly wings the focal point of the picture. The second picture depicted a peach-colored rose with a ladybug on the stem between a thorn and a leaf, and the third was a pair of salmon-colored peonies glistening with dew. All three pictures were framed in light pine frames that matched the furniture, and had pale peach backgrounds that matched the walls in the room.

On her way back to the kitchen, she paused to inspect more paintings lining the hallway. There were two paintings on each side of the hallway; two children playing with a puppy in the grass, a pair of kittens with a ball of yarn on a wooden stairway, an old man wearing spectacles and a suit with what looked like a medical bag, and a woman with a cup of tea, sitting in a rocking chair, a dreamy, faraway look in her eyes.

She arrived back in the kitchen just as Anna asked Matt how long he'd be able to stay before he left on his medical mission trip.

"I thought I'd stay until Monday," Matt replied. "I have to be in Seattle a week from tomorrow. I planned to take a couple of days to make the drive."

"How do you feel about meeting the Edwards family?" Anna inquired.

"Since Belle is going to be here, and she and Mazie have already met, I think that's a moot point, don't you?" Matt smiled. "To tell you the truth, I'm as curious about them as I'm sure they are about us. Do you have a plan for getting us all together?"

"Mazelle suggested we come over for a barbeque Friday night."

"That sounds fine to me," Matt looked at his daughter. "Belle? Are you up for meeting your biological family at a barbeque?"

"I'm a little nervous, but I want to meet them." Belle said, and then changed the subject.

"Did you do the paintings, Anna?"

"Yes, I did. It relaxes me and is something to do in my spare time." Nodding toward the closed door Belle had noticed earlier, she said, "I work in the sunroom. Take a peek if you like."

The door Anna indicated led to a glassed in room that might, at one time, have been a porch accessible from the kitchen and the dining room. All the walls were off-white and there were no curtains to obscure the view or block the light. The end of the room opposite the dining room contained a small round table set between two comfortable looking armchairs and an ottoman. The end of the room opposite the kitchen contained an easel and a workbench littered with brushes, paints and rags. A paint smock hung on a hook affixed to the wall. There was a picture in progress resting on the easel, and Belle stood in front of it for a few minutes before she returned to the kitchen and took a seat at the table.

"The sun room is amazing! It makes me wish I was artistic! I like the picture you're working on, too. Whose house is it?"

"That's Mazelle's house – where the Edwards family lives, next door. I'm going to give that picture to Mazelle for Christmas."

"It's a great house. It looks, I don't know, friendly, I guess."

"I think so, too, and I'm glad I captured that so you saw it as well." Anna smiled. Later that evening, Matt asked Anna to tell them about her house. "It's about fifty years old, I think. And it is big, but it suits my needs."

"How did you find it?" Belle asked.

"Oh, it belonged to the doctor I worked for when I first moved to Havre. He and his wife raised their four children here. His wife had chickens and a garden and a milk cow, and the kids had horses and dogs and cats. They might have even had ducks in the pond out by the barn. I'm not sure. Dr. Greyson had his office here, in the same room I use for that purpose, and he used what is now my bedroom as a place to keep overnight patients, like a mini-hospital. I worked for him for fifteen years. Of course his children were grown by then. When he retired, nobody wanted to buy this place, so he asked if I'd like to buy it, and I definitely did. His wife had passed away the year before and he was going to live with one of his daughters, so he left all the furniture, quite a few books, his old truck, and his chickens. It was a great deal for me, and it worked for him, too."

"So you still have chickens?" Matt asked, remembering Mazie and the eggs.

"Well, not the same ones, but yes," Anna laughed. "I got used to them when I first moved in here, and I liked having my own eggs. I sell a few at the farmer's market, and I trade eggs for honey with Mazelle."

"Do you still have patients?" Belle asked curiously.

"I have a few families who prefer to see me for the everyday variety of illness. More women prefer hospitals for delivering their babies now, but some still want a midwife. I delivered all of Liz's children." Anna smiled. "I guess you could say I'm easing into retirement."

"You aren't old enough to retire!" Matt objected.

"I turned sixty this year, so I might have a few good years left." Anna laughed. "Mazelle is trying to convince me to take up painting as a retirement occupation."

"If the paintings on your walls are any indication of your talent, you should deficiently do it!" Matt agreed.

Mazie burst through the kitchen door and set the eggs carefully on the kitchen table. Whirling to face Mazelle, she said breathlessly, "She's here! I saw her! And she looks just like Mom." It took a few seconds for Mazelle to grasp her meaning, and then a smile broke across her face.

"You saw Belle while you at Anna's?" she asked. Liz walked into the kitchen as Mazie nodded, still trying to catch her breath.

"What happened at Anna's?" Liz asked.

"Belle is here. She and her dad drove in just as I was leaving. Mom! She looks like you… and me." Mazie exclaimed, and then she darted to the door. "I've gotta go tell Dad."

Liz groped for a chair and sat down, a dazed look on her face. "She's here. She's really here," she murmured.

Mazelle smiled. "Perhaps you'd like to walk to Anna's tomorrow morning and have coffee? I usually go about ten."

"Do you think I should?" Liz asked anxiously.

"I think Anna will be expecting us," Mazelle replied calmly. At a questioning look from Liz, she explained further. "We thought it would be easier for Belle to meet us one or two at a time, instead all at once. At the time, I thought that you and I might have the first contact with Belle and Matt, but Mazie beat us to it."

"That's our Mazie!" Liz said with a smile and a shake of her head. Truthfully she often wished she could charge forward and tackle life the way her daughter did. Then, her thoughts turned to Belle, wondering what her personality was like, and hoping she would say and do the right things when they met the next day.

Belle sat cross-legged on the window seat, hugging a pillow to her chest and gazing moodily out the window. The blue sky and sunshine were at odds with the thoughts storming through her mind. Coming to Anna's house had been her idea. She had thought it would be a way to keep her dad from worrying about her while he was gone. Her plan had definitely not included living next door to her biological family. In fact, she was still adjusting to finding out she was adopted and that she had a biological family.

Naturally, she was curious about these relatives who had just popped into her life. Most of her friends back home had siblings, and she had often envied them their holidays and special events when everyone gathered. Maybe this was a chance to see if having grandparents, aunts, uncles, cousins, and siblings was really like she'd imagined it to be. That is, if there were, all those relatives in the Edwards family. She didn't know yet. She didn't know anything yet, really, except that Mazie seemed nice. It was the idea of another set of parents, though, that was confusing her, especially another mother.

She glanced at the clock and realized that if Mazelle and Liz weren't already sitting in the kitchen with Anna, they would be there soon. She wished she had more time think about how she felt and decide what to do. A knock sounded on the open door of her room and she looked up.

"You ready?" Matt asked.

"I don't know," Belle said with a frown. "I've been thinking."

"Have you changed your mind about meeting Mazelle and Liz?" Matt asked, looking concerned as he hesitated in the doorway. "You don't have to, you know."

"I just don't know what to do with biological parents, Dad," she blurted in frustration. "It feels funny."

"Yeah, of course."

"I liked Mazie, though," Belle said. She sighed as she set the pillow aside and stood up. "I can't avoid them all summer, so, let's go." The two of them walked down the hall and into the kitchen together.

Liz sat at the kitchen table, her coffee and banana bread untouched in front of her. Anna and Mazelle were talking, but the sound of their conversation barely penetrated her consciousness. She had dreamed of this moment since Anna took Belle out of her arms shortly after her birth. Now she waited with her heart pounding and her fists clenched in her lap, her gaze riveted on the doorway to the hall.

"Belle," she breathed, unaware that she had spoken aloud as she straightened in her chair and drank in the sight of her oldest child. Belle was dressed in yellow shorts, a white blouse and sandals, and had her blonde hair pulled back into a ponytail. She looked so much like Mazie, and yet different. She was more woman than child, slightly taller, and a little more serious, at least on this particular morning. Liz felt as if a missing piece of her heart had just fallen into place, and she wished she had the right to wrap her arms around Belle and hold her close.

Belle heard Liz whisper her name, and the sound unexpectedly touched something deep inside her, as if she remembered that voice. She chided herself at the very idea, even as her throat tightened with emotion. Maybe it was the tone she recognized, she thought frantically. It was a mother's tone, but it came from a mother who was not hers. Other than the similarity in looks, she hadn't expected to feel any kind of a connection with Liz, and the fact that she did, rattled her. She focused on Mazelle to give herself a few moments to steady her nerves.

"You are my great-grandmother?" she asked politely. Mazelle nodded with an easy smile.

"I'm delighted to see you again, Belle. You've grown into a lovely young woman."

Belle smiled her thanks at the compliment, braced herself, and turned resolutely toward Liz. "And you are my mother." She had planned to say *biological mother* but perhaps because she'd been thinking about her mom this morning, and been startled by her reaction to seeing Liz for the first time, her thoughts and her words got all tangled up.

Liz knew that any relationship she hoped to have with Belle hinged on this moment. She and Drew had talked about this meeting, about what to say and how to say it, and she was as ready as she was ever going to be, as she swallowed hard and looked directly into Belle's eyes.

"I gave birth to you, yes," Liz said, holding her voice steady with difficulty and blinking back tears. "But Debbie was your mom. I could never take her place, and I wouldn't try." Two sets of identical chocolate brown eyes stared at each other in the middle of a silence that stretched from moments to minutes. Neither of them noticed that Anna, Matt, and Mazelle had taken their coffee and slipped quietly out onto the porch.

Belle turned Liz's words over in her mind. Liz wasn't expecting to take the place of her mom? Some of the tension eased from her shoulder muscles, and she found her voice.

"I don't know what to call you," she said, dropping into the chair across the table from Liz. "And I don't know what…" she stopped talking and looked away, blushing.

"You can call me Liz." She'd been thinking about this for a long time and had her answer to Belle's unfinished question ready. "You have a right to know what I want from you, Belle, if that's what you were going to ask." Belle nodded, looking down at the table. "I want to get to know you, and I would like for us to be friends. I want to be a part of your life, if you are willing." She didn't know how she'd handle it if Belle didn't want anything to do with her, but she could only ask, because she had given up her right to demand anything from this young woman seventeen years ago. Every muscle in her body tensed as she waited for Belle to decide.

"That's what Dad said, that you and Drew probably wanted to be friends, or maybe like an aunt and uncle?"

"Yes, that's what I want. Do you want to get to know me? And Drew, and the kids?" Liz asked cautiously. "What you want is what matters and what we'll all do." She sat with her heart knocking against her ribs.

"I'm curious, and I'm here for the summer," Belle said with a little shrug. "I guess I might as well, right?" She smiled tentatively and Liz sagged with relief. It was a start, at least.

"I'm so glad!" Liz said, even as she gathered her courage to say one more thing that needed to be said. "You've just met me, Belle, but I've loved you since before you were born. It broke my heart to give you up." Belle wasn't looking at her, but Liz could see that she was listening intently.

"Drew and I, well, that was when we learned some hard lessons about being honest. I'll answer your questions whenever you want to ask them." Liz said earnestly.

"I can ask you anything?" Belle asked, looking up.

"Anything," Liz affirmed.

When Belle had first found out about being adopted, she had wondered about a lot of things, though at the moment not a single one of them came to mind, so instead she told Liz that Mazie had seemed nice and then asked about the twins.

"Thanks for giving me a second chance, Belle," Liz said softly as she stood and moved toward the door. She and Drew had talked about being patient and giving Belle the time she needed to get to know them. It was going to be hard to go slowly.

Leaving Belle alone with Liz, reminded Matt of Debbie describing Belle's first day of school; how she'd wanted to go with her, and knew she shouldn't. He felt the same way as he followed Mazelle and Anna to the porch. Belle would be fine, he assured himself, even as he worried. When Liz and Mazelle left, Matt found Belle at the kitchen table, chin in hand, lost in thought and sat down across from her.

"You okay?" he asked. "That wasn't too hard, was it?"

"I liked what Liz said about Mom."

"I did too, honey. Remember what your mom used to say about love?"

"She said there could never be too much love in this world." Belle replied with a small smile. "She also said life was an adventure. Do you think this is an adventure, Dad?"

"Could be," Matt said, trying to be positive. "You never know."

And Belle believed him, because the phrase "you never know" described her life to a T lately: death, adoption, moving, and now another family. She didn't know if she would fit in, or if she would like them, and there was no guarantee that they would like her, either. She wondered if one summer would be enough time to make some sort of sense of all the changes.

XVII

Questions & Answers

The next evening Mazie met them at the door and took charge of Belle, introducing her first to Drew and then to Wyatt and Joey who spent a lot of time looking between Liz and Mazie, as if they were seeing double. Drew did the same thing, though he was not quite so obvious about it.

"The resemblance is remarkable, isn't it?" Matt asked, noting Drew's gaze as they stood beside the grill.

"I'm glad something good came out of me being such an idiot when I left Liz. If I'd known..." Drew said, shaking his head.

"Well, if you'd known, Debbie and I wouldn't have had Belle in our lives. I suppose we would have adopted another child at some point, but I can't imagine any other child but Belle."

"I hope our two families can get to know each other now. Even with three other kids, we, especially Liz, never got over letting Belle go," Drew said.

"Debbie and I never got over the babies we lost, either, so I understand that," Matt said soberly. The two men stood silently for a few minutes, watching the twins staring at Belle.

"Drew, I'd like to talk to you privately before I leave on Monday, if I could," Matt said quietly.

"Sure. We have a few minutes before the grill is ready. We could go for a walk now." Drew suggested. Matt nodded, and the two men ambled off to the barn.

"Since I lost my wife, I've been thinking about how isolated our little family was," Matt said when they were out of earshot. "Our parents are all gone, my older sister and her husband are retired. They moved to Colorado to be near their children. Debbie had an older brother, but they were not close and I don't even know where he is. Anna is the closest family we have, and she's great, but, well, I'd like for Belle to have more of a support system." Matt stopped and looked directly at Drew, "I'm worried that if something happens to me, Belle will be all alone. I know she'll be eighteen next year, but…" his voice trailed off.

"If you're wondering if we'd be willing to look out for her if anything happened, rest assured that we would," Drew said without hesitation. "Are you comfortable with that, though? You don't really know us."

"Anna knows you, and Anna is a very good judge of character. And, although there hasn't been any contact, you are her biological family. I talked to Anna about all this last night after Belle went to bed, and she agrees. She thinks she's getting too old to be Belle's guardian. I don't want to put her on the spot," Matt said.

"Consider it done." Drew offered his hand and the two men shook on it, then they returned to the rest of the group where Wyatt and Joey were showing off Wilbur's tricks to Belle as Mazie looked on. All four of them were laughing, already comfortable with each other.

Wilbur had been a member of the family for the past three years and was actually pretty good at doing basic dog tricks. He could sit, lie down, roll over and offer his paw for a handshake most of the time. He was also worth laughing at just because of the way he looked. His fur was brown and black, and white and gray, and tan and red. He was the size of a border collie, blind in one eye, with short springy fur, one droopy ear and half his tail missing. He'd been a stray when he showed up at the back door and it quickly became obvious that the children were going to keep him. Drew had suggested they call him Mutt, but Mazie had explained, quite seriously, that calling him that would hurt his feelings, so he became Wilbur. Privately, Drew thought that the name Wilbur was harder on the ego that Mutt would have been, but he had not argued. Wilbur was a mild tempered, well-mannered dog who gave his adoration unconditionally and indiscriminately. A watch dog he was not, though Drew suspected that if a family member, specifically one of the children, was threatened, Wilber's mellow demeanor would change in the blink of an eye.

The group enjoyed hamburgers, potato salad, and watermelon and then had berry cobbler with ice cream for dessert. The evening passed pleasantly, the conversation casual and friendly.

By the time Matt left on Monday, he was feeling fairly comfortable about Belle staying with Anna and getting to know the Edwards family while he was in India.

During the next two weeks, Belle helped Anna with the housework and gardening. She also spent some time with Mazie and the boys nearly every day. They went for walks, swam in the pond, and baked cookies, while they got to know each other by asking a myriad of questions, or in the twins' case, playing silly pranks and telling bad jokes.

When Mazelle discovered that Debbie had taught her daughter to sew, she invited Belle to her sewing room. They chose fabrics and patterns and then spent several afternoons sewing a denim skirt, a pink cotton blouse, and a mint green sundress.

"All finished but the hem." Mazelle said. "If you like, we can pin that up and then all you have left is the hand sewing." Belle gave her a quizzical look and Mazelle's eyes twinkled in amusement. "Are you wondering if my old bones can sit on the floor to pin the hem for you?" She asked.

"Um, well, sort of," Belle admitted with an embarrassed shrug.

"No need for that," Mazelle assured her. "Try your dress on and then hop up on the little bench over here." As she spoke, Mazelle walked over to the corner and pulled a stool from under a triangular bench in the corner and sat down. Placing her pincushion on the floor beside her, she looked expectantly at Belle.

"I wondered what that bench was for," Belle said with a grin as she stepped up onto it. "So clever."

"My husband built everything in this sewing room for me. He had great ideas and could build anything. This is just the right height to do hems, and the corner provides support." Belle looked confused. "So if an old lady like me needed a hem measured, she wouldn't have to worry about falling off the bench with the wall so handy to lean on." Mazelle's eyes twinkled again as she began to pin up the hem.

"He thought of everything, didn't he?" Belle said.

"What he did was ask a lot of questions, listen to the answers, and then come up with brilliant ideas," Mazelle agreed.

Belle was silent for a few minutes and then she asked. "Do you have other children besides Liz's mother?"

"I have three children: James, Pete and Caroline. James was ten and Pete was seven when Caro was born. Turn just a little to your right, dear." Mazelle pinned in silence for a minute. "I had a miscarriage after Pete, and didn't think I was going to have any more children, so Caro was an extra blessing."

"How many grandchildren and great-grandchildren do you have?"

"I have eight grandchildren. James had James Junior, Rob and Mary, Pete had Sara and Lucy, and Caro had Liz, Adam and John. Then there are nineteen greats; Will was almost two when you were born. He has a sister, Rachael. The others are Emily and David, Marcus, Paul and Ann Marie, Seth and Diane, Alison and Daniel, Mazie, Joey and Wyatt, Bob and Bill, Rebecca and Patrick." Mazelle finished her list of names as she put the last pin in the hem. She stood and offered a hand as Belle stepped down from the bench.

"I was counting, and that's only eighteen," Belle said. Mazelle put the pincushion back on the table and turned to face her.

"Liz had a feeling you were a girl. She named you Belle before you were born. I was there when she felt you kick for the first time. I helped make the clothes we sent with you to your new home. I watched her struggle with the decision to give you up, and saw how carefully she chose your parents. I was there when Anna delivered you. I held you while Anna tended to Liz, and then helped clean you up and dress you in a little green gown almost the same color as this sundress. I've loved you and prayed for you every day since, and I always count you as one of my greats, Belle. Always," she said softly.

"Oh," Belle said as she blinked back tears.

"Aunt Anna, do you think Liz meant it when she said she'd answer my questions?" Belle asked that evening over supper.

"Of course. Haven't you asked her anything yet?"

"Not really. They are going to paint her classroom over the summer, so she's been getting all her stuff packed into boxes. I haven't had a chance to ask her anything. When I first found out I was adopted, I had a million questions, but now I can't decide where to start." Belle shrugged.

"Maybe it would help to make a list?" Anna suggested.

"That'd be weird. I'd feel dumb pulling out my list and starting with number one."

"I didn't mean like that," Anna laughed. "I meant that if you wrote things down, it might help you to organize your thoughts and figure out what you wanted to know first. Maybe you could even group your questions into topics so you could talk about one thing at a time."

"Oh. Yeah, that makes sense. I might try it."

That evening in her room, Belle jotted down a list of things she was curious about and she was thinking about them when she arrived at the Edwards house the next day, joining the three children and Wilbur on the porch.

"Belle!" Wyatt shouted. "Guess what! Everyone will be here for the 4th!"

"Oh?" Belle replied, absently, still thinking about what she wanted to ask Liz. "Who is everyone?"

"All the grandparents, and Zeke and John and maybe even Adam." Wyatt rattled off excitedly. Joey noticed that Belle wasn't smiling and he interrupted his brother to explain.

"We have a family reunion on the 4th of July. You'll meet the rest of the family," he stopped, looking uncertain. "I mean, if you want to."

Mazie looked anxiously at Belle and added her comments. "We didn't think they were going to be able to make it but Mom just got a letter that they can come after all." Belle looked from Wyatt to Joey to Mazie, still without speaking.

"I have to go," she said at last. She turned on her heel, stepped off the porch and walked rapidly back down the driveway. By the time she got to the road, she was running, tears streaming down her face. She did not stop until she was safely in her room with the door closed. Then she sank onto the bed and wrapped her arms around her middle, sobbing and gasping for breath, and she cried for a long time.

Anna was weeding the garden when Wyatt, Joey and Mazie found her. She glanced up smiling, but sobered at the looks on their faces. "What is it?" she asked.

"Belle." Joey answered, but then he shrugged helplessly, at a loss for words.

"It's me and my big mouth," Wyatt explained grimly. "I told her about our family reunion and..." his voice trailed off.

Mazie finished, "We were all talking and whatever we said made Belle cry and she ran home."

"Ah," Anna said, nodding in understanding. "Well, sometimes we need to cry, to let the sadness out."

"What?" Joey asked.

"Belle is still sad because her mother died. So she needs to let that sadness out."

"Oh," Joey said.

"I'll check on her. Don't worry," Anna soothed the children. They gave her dubious looks and turned to go back home. Anna continued to weed the garden until it was time for lunch. She found Belle in the kitchen fixing sandwiches. Her eyes were red, her hands shook slightly, and her face was pale, but she seemed composed.

"The Edwards children stopped by to check on you. They seem to think they made you cry," Anna said as they sat down to eat.

"I cried, yeah, but it wasn't their fault." Anna didn't say anything and after a moment, Belle tried to explain, "They have company coming for the 4th. A family reunion, they said. And all of a sudden it hit me that I don't have grandparents, my dad is in India and I miss my mom. Next thing I knew I was crying and I couldn't stop."

"It makes sense that hearing about their family would make you think about yours. You miss your mom, and of course you miss your dad, too, since he's been gone two weeks."

"Yeah," Belle agreed, and then muttered. "So now I have red eyes and a headache. I just hate to cry! And I'm not good at it."

"I don't think anybody's *good* at it, but somehow it helps ease heartache," Anna said matter-of-factly. "The thing is that the kids think you're upset about their reunion. Are you?"

"Maybe a little. I like them, but they aren't my family, are they?" Belle asked miserably.

"Technically, they are your blood relatives, but you just met them, so they don't feel like family just yet. Whether you want them to be your family on an emotional level is something you haven't had time to figure out." Anna said kindly. "Don't worry about it, I'm sure things will work out if you just relax and take your time."

Belle's tears were the topic of conversation at the supper table in the Edwards house that evening. The children explained to Mazelle and their parents what had transpired on the porch and how badly they felt about making Belle cry.

"I'm sure you didn't mean to upset her," Liz began. "Maybe all the talk about family just overwhelmed her. Remember that she lost her mom not so long ago."

"That's what Anna said," Joey reported. "She said Belle needs to let the sadness out."

"Yeah, and she said crying does that. Is that why you cry?" Wyatt looked at his mother.

"Sometimes," she said with a smile. "And don't forget, she recently found out about being adopted and that we live next door to Anna. She's also in a new place and her dad is far away, so that's a lot of big changes in a short amount of time."

"I think your mom is right," Drew agreed. "Belle might need some breathing room. And that means that if she doesn't want to meet all the relatives, we don't push her. Agreed?" Everyone nodded soberly.

"Has Belle asked you any questions?" Drew asked, later that night. Liz shook her head.

"No, I've been expecting her to, but she seems to be almost avoiding me," Liz said sadly. "She gets along with the kids, and she's been sewing with Grandma, but..." her voice trailed off.

"I don't think it's you, Lizzie. She lost her mom and then found out she had another mother. It's confusing... I've been thinking." Drew said. "Do you think it would help if she read our journals? Maybe she doesn't know exactly what to ask."

"That might help," Liz said. "If I can figure out a way to bring it up. I can't just shove them into her hands and say 'here, read these.'"

"No," Drew agreed pulling her into his arms and giving her a hug. "We can't rush things, but I think you will be able to bring it up to her one of these days. We have to be patient like we told the kids to be." Liz nodded.

The next morning, Liz was sitting at the kitchen table sipping coffee and making notes about the upcoming family reunion when Belle knocked at the door.

"Good morning, Belle," Liz said. "The kids are helping with Vacation Bible School at the church. Sorry you missed them."

"I know. That's where Anna is, too. She's the snack lady today, I think. I came to talk to you, if you aren't busy or anything."

"I always have time for you, Belle. Do you want coffee? I noticed you drank some with your dad." Belle nodded.

"Anna said Mazie and the boys were worried they made me cry yesterday, and they didn't." Belle said, once they were seated at the table.

"Oh?" Liz sipped her coffee and waited.

"I just all of a sudden really missed my mom," Belle said with her eyes on her coffee cup.

"The kids will be relieved to hear that they didn't cause your tears. We explained to them that you've had a lot of big changes in your life and that could make you extra sensitive." She paused, and then added, "I'm really sorry about your mom, wish I could've met her."

"You would have liked her," Belle agreed softly. "And she would have liked you, I think." She looked at Liz's notes. "What are you doing?"

"I'm trying to figure out where everyone will sleep and jot down some ideas for meals."

"Wyatt and Joey said all of their grandparents are coming. How many grandparents do they have?" Belle asked curiously.

"Let's see, there are my parents, Phil and Caroline, and Drew's parents, John and Jean, and Grandpa Joe, he's Drew's grandpa on his dad's side. Grandma Mazelle is my mother's mom."

Belle digested this, and said, "I don't have any grandparents. Well, I mean my mom and dad's parents all died a long time ago, so I don't remember them." She stared into space and then asked tentatively, "So, um, biologically, those people are my grandparents and great-grandparents, too?"

"Yes, and they are all a little nervous about meeting you," Liz laughed.

"Nervous? Why?" Belle asked in surprise.

"Well, to be honest, they would love to claim you as part of the family. They are worried you won't like them or that you won't want them to be your grandparents."

"Oh," It made her feel a little better that she wasn't the only one who was nervous about meeting new relatives. She changed the subject. "I was talking to Grandma

Mazelle while we were sewing and she told me the names of all her kids and grandkids and great grandkids, so I know Adam and John are your brothers, but who is Zeke?" Liz was thrilled to hear Belle refer to Mazelle as *grandma* but she didn't comment on that as she answered the question.

"Zeke is the son of Drew's sister, Trish and her husband Luke. He's a year younger than Wyatt and Joey. They also have a daughter, Maggie, who is a year younger than Mazie."

"Oh. All of them live in Shelby?"

"My parents live in town, and Drew's parents live on the farm. Luke and Trish live on the farm, too."

"Where do your brothers live?"

"Adam and his family live in Great Falls. That's about ninety miles from Shelby. He's an insurance agent, and Lynn works part-time in his office. They have two boys, Bobby is ten and Billy is eight." Liz took a sip of coffee and then continued. "John and his family live in Fort Benton. John and Kate are both teachers. They have a boy and a girl. Rebecca is eight and Daniel is six."

"It's hard to get used to where things are in a different state," Belle said. "I kind of know where Great Falls is, but where is Fort Benton?"

"Fort Benton is about forty miles from Great Falls, almost a hundred miles from Shelby, and about seventy-five miles from here. I think of it as an inverted triangle – Shelby on one side, Havre on the other, and Great Falls on the bottom, kind of between the two, with Fort Benton just above Great Falls."

"Besides remembering where the towns are, and how far they are from here, I'll never be able to keep all the names and ages straight!" Belle exclaimed. "I'll need to carry a chart with me and I might ask everyone to wear a name tag."

"Not a bad idea," Liz laughed. "So, I hope that means you're willing to meet them?"

"Well, I'll have to, otherwise the twins will think I'm a chicken. Plus, I'm curious. I've been an only child for so long, so it's a bit strange to have so many relatives all of a sudden."

"I'm sure it is," Liz sympathized.

"It's kind of exciting in a way, too." Belle admitted. "So where do you put everyone?"

"Usually my parents and Drew's parents stay in the kids' rooms, and we put a bed in the sewing room for Grandpa Joe. Trish and Luke will probably sleep in the living room, and Adam and Lynn and John and Kate can use the two rooms of the bunk-house. All the kids, ours included, can sleep out there, too, in the bunks."

"Are there enough bunks? I thought there were six extra kids, plus Mazie and the twins. I only counted eight bunks when I was in the bunkhouse with Mazie last week."

"You probably didn't notice that there are two trundle beds under the bunks by the windows, so there are ten beds. I have to tell you, I thought both Grandma and Drew were a little crazy when they did that remodeling project during Drew's last year of college. But Grandma said we needed to be looking toward the future. And we've used it for other things besides the occasional family gathering."

"Like what?" Belle wanted to know.

"Last year the church had a visiting choir and we housed them here. We've had other people's families for weddings and funerals and one year we housed a bunch of stranded travelers during a blizzard. That space gets used several times a year."

"Wow. How do you feed all those people?" Belle asked.

"Usually other people pitch in to feed them, since we are providing shelter. The church will have a potluck or families will take turns providing meals."

"When you have family here, do they all help with meals, then?"

"Once people are here, everyone pitches in to help, but first there has to be a plan. That's the hard part, and that's what I'm working on today. I'm trying to come up with ideas for what to cook." Belle nodded, lost in thought. Liz let her be, reading through her notes again and making a couple of additions.

"My dad said I'm lucky to have another family and that I should get to know ev-eryone," Belle said at last.

"I'm glad your dad doesn't mind sharing you. But what do you think?"

"I like everyone. It's strange to go from having a small family to having such a big one."

"Glad to hear that you like everyone," Liz said. "And, I wanted to remind you that I'm willing to answer any questions you might have about my decision to put you up for adoption."

Belle looked uncomfortable. Liz waited patiently, and finally Belle said, "I guess I just don't know what to ask."

"Drew and I talked about this the other night," Liz said slowly. "When he came to see me after the war and wanted to get back together, I had trouble talking about it.

To be honest, I had trouble even listening to him try to talk about it. Everything was all mixed up in my mind, like a jigsaw puzzle. I couldn't get the pieces sorted so I could put the picture together. Is that how you feel?"

"That's it exactly!" Belle exclaimed, nodding. "You guys obviously figured it out, what did you do?"

"I didn't do anything. My natural inclination is to run and hide from problems." Liz sighed. "I hope I'm getting better about that with time." She shook her head ruefully.

"But anyway, Drew did take action. He sent me his journal and a letter begging me to read it."

"In the mail?"

"Yes, I think he knew that if he just handed it to me, I wouldn't take it or read it. I might not have read it anyway if Grandma hadn't seen me with it and given me one of her stern looks."

"She was on Drew's side?" Belle asked in surprise.

"She just thought he should know about you and that he should hear it from me."

"So you read the journal, and then you talked?" Belle asked with a sympathetic smile.

"Not exactly," Liz sighed. "I read the journal and I told him I'd read it, but I still couldn't tell him about you. I knew he had a right to know, but it just hurt too much and I couldn't do it."

"So what happened?"

"When he got ready to leave that weekend, I put my journal in with his, using the mailing envelope he sent me, and gave it to him. It was a spur of the moment decision and, well, I didn't tell him I'd given him my journal." Liz shook her head again and smiled ruefully.

"So he thought you were just returning his journal," Belle mused. "How long did it take for him to find yours and read it?" she asked with a little smirk.

Liz rolled her eyes. "Over two weeks."

"Wow," Belle said.

"I know. I made things way more complicated than they needed to because I was such a coward. But getting back to the present, I've been trying to put myself in your place. I was about your age when all this started and it occurred to me that you've come into the middle of a story, so to speak. Drew suggested that I let you read our journals. That would give you all the background, and then we could talk. Do you think that would help?"

"A journal is private, right? Has anyone else read them?"

"Yes, they are very personal. I mentioned mine to Grandma and my mom, and Drew talked to his parents about his and he told them he'd read mine, but nobody else has ever read them." Liz replied. "They don't concern anyone else, except you."

"I think I would like to read them," Belle said after thinking for a few moments. Liz got up from the table and left the kitchen, returning in a few minutes with a flat parcel, which she handed to Belle.

"After you read them, both Drew and I will be happy to answer any questions you might have." Brave words, she thought to herself, even as she said them. She was a nervous wreck worrying about Belle's reaction to those journals, especially hers.

XVIII

Filling in the Blanks

Belle walked home deep in thought, the two journals clutched to her chest. When she reached the house she went directly to her room and laid the two notebooks side by side on the desk. She looked at them for several minutes without opening either one. Then she went into the kitchen.

When Anna got home from serving snacks and cleaning up the church kitchen at Vacation Bible School, she found Belle in the kitchen taking a pan of brownies out of the oven.

"Well, this is a nice surprise. There's nothing better than the smell of warm chocolate!"

"Actually, I think the taste of warm chocolate is better than the smell of it!" Belle protested, smiling over her shoulder as she stirred a pot on the stove.

"True!" Anna laughed. "And I am still not caught up on my chocolate consumption from when we couldn't get it during the war. What else did you make?"

"Chicken noodle soup," Belle replied.

"Comfort food?" Anna asked.

"I guess so. Cooking helps me think." She put the spoon down and turned to face Anna. "I went over to talk to Liz this morning, and as soon as I was sitting at the table with her, every question I wrote down last night in my room went right out of my head." Anna nodded encouragement and started to set the table as Belle talked.

"We ended up talking about the reunion and who was coming and where they would sleep and all of that. Then Liz asked if I had any questions for her and I just told her I couldn't think where to start, so she told me a little about when Drew came back from the war, and how she couldn't even talk to him because things were so mixed up in her mind."

"Yes, she was very sad during that time."

"She said that she and Drew had talked about it and Drew thought if I read their journals, it would help." Anna stopped arranging silverware on the table and turned to stare at Belle.

"Really? They offered to let you read their journals?"

Belle nodded. "Liz gave them to me." She brought bowls of soup to the table. "That's a big deal, isn't it? I mean when you are writing in a journal, you don't expect anyone else to ever read it, so you put down whatever you are thinking or feeling. It's totally honest."

"Yes, it is. Letting someone read your innermost thoughts and feelings is like handing them your heart," Anna said, sitting down to eat. "When are you going to read them?"

"I'm trying to decide which one to read first."

"Maybe you should read them at the same time," Anna suggested. "Read part of one and then part of the other. They'll probably have dates, so you can go in order that way." Belle nodded thoughtfully and said that might be a good idea.

She retired to her room after they ate and started reading the journals, switching back and forth between the two as Anna had suggested, very glad she knew there was eventually a happy ending to this story. She empathized with Liz as a pregnant teen and with Drew as a soldier. When she finished, she wiped tears from her face and glanced at the clock, surprised to see that it was nearly eight in the morning. She'd been so immersed in the history of her biological parents that she hadn't realized she'd read through the night. She found Anna in the sunroom, contemplating a blank canvas.

"Am I disturbing you?" she asked tentatively.

"Quite the contrary, dear," Anna looked relieved. "I was beginning to worry about you and thought a bit of painting would occupy my mind. But I couldn't get into the mood to paint. Shall we have breakfast?" Belle said she was hungry and they headed for the kitchen.

"I just finished the journals," Belle said as they ate. "I feel like I cried my way through them."

"It was a very hard time for both of them. Are you glad you read them?"

"Yes, but I feel like I lived through those two years with both of them. I'm exhausted!"

"You were up all night, you should take a nap, dear," Anna said kindly.

When she had finished her tea and toast, Belle did just that and slept until early afternoon. She awoke refreshed and decided to go and talk to Liz. As she passed the barn, though, she saw that Drew was there and on impulse she stopped beside the tractor.

"Hey, Belle. How are you today?" Drew asked when he saw her standing there.

"I was up all night reading the journals," Belle replied, shifting nervously from one foot to the other. "So then I took a nap after breakfast and I just got up."

"I think Lizzie and I both stayed up all night reading each other's journals, too." Drew said seriously, searching her face. "Do you want to ask me anything? Or maybe smack me?" Belle shook her head and gave him a small smile.

"No." She took a deep breath and looked him in the eye. "I want to thank you for letting me read them. It was like living through everything that happened right along with you and Liz, and it made me realize that it was just a hard time for both of you." Drew nodded, stared into space for a minute then looked back at her and spoke in a husky voice.

"I've always felt like it was my fault Lizzie had to give you up, Belle. If I hadn't broken up with her, she would have told me she was pregnant and we could have gotten married right away. Then she could have kept you. You would have been ours."

"Yes, but I ended up with great parents. Mom and Dad couldn't have children of their own. So something good came of it, right?" Belle choked out, her eyes shining with tears. Drew nodded and held his arms out in invitation. Belle accepted his hug gratefully as she sobbed against his chest. Neither of them saw or heard Joey and Wyatt approach the barn, stop in their tracks, back up slowly until they were out of earshot and then sprint toward the house.

"Mom!" they called as they burst through the kitchen door. "Belle is crying in the barn."

"Oh no!" Liz exclaimed. "What happened? Is she hurt?"

"We were going to see if Dad needed some help," said Joey. "And we saw Belle talking to him and then right when we were almost there, he held out his arms and she just started crying all over him."

"Yeah," Wyatt said. "And she sounded like there was a lot of sadness coming out."

"What?" Liz asked in bewilderment.

"Anna said that sometimes you have to cry to let your sadness out, remember?" Wyatt explained. "We told you that."

"So Dad is with her?" Liz asked.

"Yeah, and she's crying all over him," Joey repeated. Mazie had come into the room in time to hear most of the recitation by the twins. She looked at her mother.

"If she's crying with Dad, that's better than crying by herself, right?"

"Your dad has a great shoulder for crying on." Liz agreed, but she looked worried.

Belle cried for a long time while Drew patted her back and murmured his sympathy. His own eyes were wet and his throat was tight when her sobs ceased. She took a shuddering breath before she stepped back.

"I'm sorry. I got your shirt all wet."

"It's okay. In fact, I'm glad." Drew replied. At her surprised look, he went on. "I'm sorry for your pain, but I'm glad you are here, glad you read the journals, and relieved that you don't hate me." He paused. "I know you already have a great dad, but I'm hoping you get to a place where you consider us part of your family, too."

"I think I'm already there," Belle confided with a watery smile. Drew smiled and suggested they go and see Liz. They walked to the house side by side and found Liz in the kitchen with Mazelle, fixing supper. Drew took Belle by the hand, walked over to Liz and took her hand. Placing Belle's hand in Liz's hand, he said simply, "Belle read our journals." Then he stepped back as Liz and Belle hugged each other, both of them crying. Just then Wyatt and Joey walked into the kitchen.

"Dad," Joey whispered. "Belle was crying in the barn and now she's crying here. What is going on?"

"Its girl stuff, son," Drew whispered back. He went to the cookie jar, grabbed a handful of oatmeal cookies and motioned the boys to follow him. Once they were out of the kitchen, he handed each of them two cookies and said, "You two are men, so you need to know that girls cry when they're sad, and sometimes when they're happy."

"So is Belle happy or sad?" Wyatt wanted to know, munching his cookie.

"A little of both, I think," Drew replied.

"And what about Mom?" Joey asked, as he contemplated the cookies in his hands. "Is her crying a little of both, too?" Drew nodded.

"Why did you give us cookies right before supper?" Joey wanted to know.

"Supper might be a little late," Drew said with a smile as he took a bite out of the cookie in his own hand. "I didn't want you to starve."

Belle stayed for supper, and afterwards, she and Liz talked in the kitchen for over an hour. At first they talked about Liz's journal, but before long, Belle spoke about her own mom.

"She loved to cook and sew, and she had a green thumb. But mostly, she was good at explaining stuff," Belle remembered. "I still don't know why she didn't explain the adoption to me. I've heard that sometimes people tell their kids about being adopted when they are little. They do it like a fairy tale, you know, and explain that the parents wanted a child so much and searched for just the right one. I wonder why she didn't do something like that."

"Was your mom sick, Belle?" Liz asked.

"I never thought about it, I guess. She had lots of days when she didn't have much energy, but other days she felt fine. It didn't seem to matter because she was almost always happy." Belle replied. "Why did you ask that?"

"Anna told Mazelle that Debbie was rather frail. She thought maybe that contributed to her having so many miscarriages, or that having the miscarriages damaged her health. Hard to say which came first," Liz answered.

"But what does that have to do with telling me about being adopted?" Belle asked.

"This is just my opinion, and we'll never know for sure, okay?" Belle nodded. "Well, I've been trying to see things from her point of view. It seems to me that your mom was a very intelligent, very intuitive woman, so it is possible she had a feeling she might die young. If that were the case, if she knew or suspected her time with you was limited, maybe she just didn't want to upset the happy family life you had together."

Belle digested this, chin in hand, gazing toward the window. After a moment or two, she nodded slowly and smiled. "You know, sometimes she just sort of 'knew' things, so that would make sense. She liked for everyone to get along, and maybe she thought I'd be upset about being adopted." Belle shrugged. "Dad said they agreed to tell me when I was younger, but Mom always changed her mind. The next deadline was supposed to be on my eighteenth birthday, but she didn't make it that long." Belle looked serious for a minute, and then grinned. "When Dad finally told me, he said, 'Your mother and I couldn't have children.' So I said I knew where babies came from and that the stork didn't bring me. He got all flustered and nervous, and finally told me everything from the beginning." Belle giggled. "If Mom saw that from heaven, she was laughing at him, for sure."

Liz treasured the new, more relaxed relationship she had with Belle, and couldn't wait for her parents and Drew's parents to meet her when they came for the reunion and Mazelle's birthday. It was similar to the way she had felt when their parents had come to see each of the children right after they were born.

XIX

Reunions

Since the 4th of July fell on a Tuesday, the family reunion was to last the whole week. Caro and Phil Baxter arrived on Saturday morning and were all unpacked by the time John and Jean Edwards and Grandpa Joe arrived that afternoon. Liz had invited Anna and Belle for supper, hoping it would be less overwhelming to meet the family in small groups.

Belle arrived with a pan of brownies, and Anna had a bowl of coleslaw to serve with the fried chicken and mashed potatoes Mazelle and Liz had fixed. Once they put the food away, they followed Liz onto the front porch where everyone was visiting. She made the introductions and Belle was amazed at how quickly she felt at ease with her biological grandparents and Great-Grandpa Joe. She thought it probably had something to do with Liz telling her they were nervous about meeting her, too. It put them on a more equal footing, in her mind, at least. Everyone seemed thrilled to meet her. She was getting used to meeting new relatives she hadn't known about, and she was also getting used to the comments about how much she resembled Liz and Mazie. Both of her grandmothers asked her questions about school and her Dad's medical mission to India, shared anecdotes about themselves and their grandchildren, and wanted to know how she liked Montana so far.

"I really like it here," Belle answered. "Everyone has been so nice to me, and I like the area. I've been thinking I might want to move here."

"That would be wonderful, dear! Then we could see you more often. Maybe you could even go to college here when you finish high school." Caro was the first to recover the power of speech, but Jean flashed a broad smile and nodded her agreement.

"I just might," Belle told her with a twinkle in her eye. "But I haven't discussed it with Dad or Anna yet."

"I'd love to have you, Belle, you know that." Anna smiled at her, and the conversation moved on to other topics.

Adam and John and their families and Luke and Trish and their children arrived on Sunday. Mazie and the twins led their cousins to the bunkhouse and there was much laughing and joking around while each of them chose a bed and got settled.

"When do we get to meet Belle?" Maggie asked. "I heard she looks like you and your mom. Is she nice?"

"She's great, you'll like her." Mazie replied.

"Well, is she our cousin for real, or is she a friend of the family, or what?" Maggie asked.

"We aren't supposed to push her on stuff like that. Everyone thinks she needs time to decide. But last night she said she likes it here and might want to move here, so I think that means she might be pretty close to being family." Mazie confided. "Okay. I'll keep my fingers crossed and try not to say the wrong thing," Maggie said.

Belle and Anna had offered to bring fresh garlic bread to go with the spaghetti Liz and her mother were making for supper. It was delicious, and Belle had an instant rapport with Maggie, Zeke and Bobby. The younger kids didn't seem to notice or care that Belle was a new addition to their family. Belle thought that might be the difference between six and eight-year-olds and ten, eleven and twelve-year-olds.

Mazelle looked around in happy satisfaction the next evening. The women had cleaned up the kitchen after the men cooked a pancake supper for everyone. They always made a big mess, but they had fun and it was such a joy to see fathers and sons of all ages working together that nobody cared. And the pancakes and bacon and eggs were delicious.

The women had spent the day in the sewing room assembling and tying two crazy quilts. Each of them contributed several sections they had put together at home. They did a project like this every year and then donated whatever they made to charity. Some years they made baby quilts for hospitals, but this year Kate knew of a family who had lost everything in a fire. In addition to the quilt, each family had collected a box of children's clothing. John and Kate would take everything home with them and see that it got to the family in need.

Now the adults were having tea and coffee on the porch and the children were playing charades in the living room. Belle had been visiting with Adam and Lynn earlier, and was now deep in conversation with John and Kate. Earlier that afternoon, while they were in the sewing room, she had shown everyone the clothes they had made together. She was fitting in just fine, as Mazelle had known she would if she relaxed and gave herself a chance. And the family had welcomed her with open arms and loving hearts. Mazelle had known that would happen, too.

Drew, Adam and John manned the grill to cook hamburgers and hot dogs on the 4th of July. Liz, Lynn and Kate insisted that Mazelle relax and visit with them while they spent the morning making potato salad and apple pie. While the meat was cooking, they sliced tomatoes and onions, cut up watermelon and set the table. The older kids had a game of croquet going on the lawn, and the younger kids were playing tag. When it got dark, everyone sat on the porch where they had a great view of the fireworks display sponsored by the Lions Club at the county fairgrounds, and then everyone enjoyed apple pie and homemade ice cream before bed.

Wednesday, the men and some of the boys went fishing and came back with enough fish for supper. They wrapped the fish in foil and cooked it on the grill. Caro and Jean prepared fresh red potatoes, green beans from the garden, and cornbread. Belle thought it was delicious, and she had not, to this point, considered herself a fish lover. There was angel food cake, well, two angel food cakes – one with frosting and one without, for dessert because they were celebrating Grandma Mazelle's birthday.

Thursday Caro and Jean put a turkey in the oven and that night they enjoyed a Thanksgiving type feast with all the trimmings. This was traditional for their summer reunion. Belle soon learned to put names and faces together, and enjoyed her new grandparents, aunts, uncles, and cousins. Being part of a big family was turning out to be everything she had imagined it to be.

Friday everyone had the leftover of their choice for supper. There was plenty of noise as both children and adults called dibs on the spaghetti, or hot dogs or hamburgers. There was some complaining from Grandpa Joe that nobody had told him about the turkey pot pie and that was his favorite, but Grandma Jean said she'd put dibs on it for him, so he was happy. Whoever yelled first got that leftover, though there didn't seem to be a shortage, and nobody went hungry. Afterwards, they watched a skit and a song and dance routine that the children had worked on all week. They performed while the bonfire was getting started, and then everyone got to roast marshmallows and make s'mores for dessert. Saturday everyone was up early to clean up, get packed and start home.

"It's sad when they all leave, isn't it?" Belle asked as the last car drove away.

"Yes, but it was sure fun while they were here." Mazie said. "All the cousins gave you their vote of approval, in case you were wondering."

"Did they?" Belle said. She had been wondering what they thought about her. "I liked them, too."

XX

Another New Beginning

Matt wondered what he'd find when he got to Anna's house. The medical mission had gone well and he believed that he and his team had accomplished a lot, not only with the people for whom they had provided medical care, but also in establishing connections and building a foundation for future trips to the same area. His mind drifted back over the events of the past few months. When the idea had been conceived, and they started planning the mission, he had accepted that he would not be able to communicate with his family for two months. He and Debbie had talked about it and agreed to those conditions because they both believed in the mission.

It had been more difficult than he had imagined to be totally cut off from Belle. He wondered if he'd find her as listless as she'd been when he left two months ago. His own grief was starting to ease, but he admitted to himself that he was not looking forward to returning to Laramie and confronting all the memories he and Debbie had created there. In fact, he had been toying with the idea of relocating, if not immediately, then after Belle graduated from high school next year.

When the plane landed in Seattle, Matt found a pay phone and dialed Anna's number. He let it ring a long time, but nobody answered. He tried again after he retrieved his luggage, but there was still no answer. He picked up his car, loaded his luggage and paid the storage fee. At the gas station where he filled the tank, he found another pay phone and called a third time, with the same result.

As Matt navigated out of the airport and through the city, he ran through the possibilities in his mind. It was mid-morning in Havre, so maybe they were in the garden, or running errands, or visiting the Edwards family. The little voice in his mind reminded him that they knew he was arriving in Seattle today, and would be expecting him to call. He hoped nothing was wrong. He had slept for several hours on the overnight flight, so he started driving east, stopping for a sandwich in Spokane. There he found a phone and called again, but there was still no answer.

"Belle!" Anna exclaimed when they came into the kitchen and she caught sight of the calendar. Mazelle's apple tree had produced a bumper crop of apples this year and the two of them had spent the day helping to make jars of apple butter and applesauce, and a half dozen apple pies for each family to put in the freezer.

"What?" Belle asked as she put down the box she was carrying. She followed Anna's gaze to the calendar, and gasped. "Oh no! Dad probably tried to call and is wondering why we didn't answer."

"I'm sorry, dear, I was so focused on helping Mazelle that I completely forgot what day it was. I hope he isn't worried. One of us needs to stay near the phone." As she spoke, the phone rang and Belle snatched it up.

"Hello?" she said.

"Belle!" Matt's relieved voice came over the wire. "How are you, honey? I was starting to get worried when I couldn't reach you."

"Sorry, Dad, we spent the day with Grandma Mazelle and Liz. Are you still in Seattle?"

"No, I slept on the plane, so I drove today. I'm staying overnight in Missoula, so I'll be there tomorrow." They chatted for a few minutes more, but mindful of the long distance charges, didn't linger on the phone. Matt breathed a sigh of relief as he walked to the restaurant located next door to his motel. Belle had referred to Mazelle as grandma and spent the day with her and Liz working in the kitchen. That sounded like a good sign. He slept easy that night, in spite of the noise from the highway, and woke refreshed for the day-long drive to Havre.

Belle waited excitedly for her dad to get there and spotted his car turning into Anna's driveway just as they were putting supper on the table. Matt had barely stepped out of the car when Belle hurled herself into his arms with a muffled, "I missed you, Dad!" Matt hugged her tight and whispered that he had missed her, too, and then they went into the kitchen where Anna had a big bowl of homemade soup and a chicken sandwich already on the table for him. He hugged Anna and the three of them sat down to eat.

Matt paid close attention to his daughter over the next few days and was relieved to see that Belle seemed to have her sparkle back. She smiled easily and often and interacted with the Edwards family and with Anna as if she'd lived there forever. These things encouraged him to present the idea he'd been turning over in his mind. The opportunity came the next morning over coffee and apple coffee cake.

"You've had a good summer here, haven't you?" he asked Belle.

"Yeah, it's been great. Everyone has been so nice and I got to meet a bunch of people in the family over the 4th of July. There were six of my cousins and three sets of aunts and uncles, a great-grandpa, and two sets of grandparents! I want you to meet them all, Dad. They treated me like I'd always been a part of their family."

"Are you an official part of the family then?" Matt asked, his eyes twinkling.

"I guess so," she replied, and then she sobered. "I still miss Mom a lot. But it helps to have so many people who care about me. Grandma Mazelle helped me sew some new clothes, and Liz and Drew let me read their journals so I could see why things happened the way they did. Mazie and I are great friends, and the boys treat me like a big sister. Even Wilbur likes me."

"Are you ready to go back home to Laramie?" Matt asked, trying to be casual, as he waited for her reply.

She was quiet for several minutes, chewing on her lip, and finally she shook her head and said softly, "Not really. I wish I could stay here."

"I'm glad to hear that."

Belle looked at him in surprise. "You are?"

"Yes. I've been thinking that a new place to live might be a good idea for both of us. We are never going to forget your mother, but there are so many memories in Laramie that I don't really want to live there anymore. I would be willing to go back for your last year in high school if you wanted to…"

"Dad! Let's stay here!" Belle exclaimed. "Anna already said I could stay with her as long as I wanted. I can go to school here, and there's a college here too!" Belle jumped out of her chair and did a little dance around the kitchen. Matt smiled as he watched her, and he knew both their hearts were on the mend.

The next few weeks flew by as Matt made arrangements to pack up their household things and move them to Havre. They accepted Anna's invitation to live with her, at least for Belle's senior year. There was plenty of room in the barn to store their furniture and whatever else they did not need.

Matt gave notice at the hospital in Laramie and put his application in at the Havre Hospital, where it was immediately accepted. While he was busy with those things, Belle registered at the high school, filling out the paperwork to have her school records transferred. In no time at all, Matt was working and it was time for Belle to start school.

Belle thought Havre High School would be the same as the high school in Laramie, but it wasn't. Havre High School was a lot smaller, and it seemed like everyone knew everyone else. When she pre-registered and filled out the paperwork to have her school records transferred, she'd dealt with a summer helper. On the first day of school, however, she came face to face with the school secretary.

"My name is Belle Jackson, I'm new. I filled out papers a couple of weeks ago to have my school records transferred from Laramie, Wyoming."

"My word! For a minute I thought you were Mazie Edwards. You look exactly like her!" The secretary exclaimed with wide eyes.

"Yes, well, we are sisters." Belle replied. She hadn't planned to say that. She hadn't thought about what to say at all, but once the words were out of her mouth, she decided she didn't mind. Maybe it was odd to have two families, but this was the start of the sixties, people could adjust, and as Grandma Mazelle said, the truth was better than a lie.

"Sisters?" the secretary said, looking confused. "I thought Mazie was the oldest."

"Oh, she is the oldest in her family. I was adopted and grew up as an only child. My dad is Dr. Matt Jackson. He just started work at the hospital here." Belle was starting to enjoy this. The poor school secretary looked shocked. "We live next door to the Edwards family, with Dad's aunt, Anna Winslow."

"I see. Well, let's get you registered and on your way to class, young lady." She looked through a pile of papers, found Belle's schedule and her new student packet and sent her on her way. Belle thought the woman was glad to be rid of her.

Throughout the day, most of the teachers and about half of the students gave her the same surprised look when she introduced herself, though nobody else asked her any rude questions.

"How was your first day, dear?" Anna asked when Belle got home.

"Interesting. Very interesting."

"In what way?" Anna wanted to know. So Belle explained what had happened when she went to the office that morning and the looks she had gotten throughout the day.

"I'm so used to the resemblance that I didn't think about it, and it took me by surprise. When the secretary gave me the third degree, I just decided it would be better to answer all her questions. I didn't know what else to do."

"Maybe we should share this with Liz and Drew," Anna said, and the two of them walked over to the Edwards home.

"Come in!" Mazelle said, opening the door and stepping back to let them enter. "The kids are having an after-school snack in the kitchen."

"Maybe they should hear this, too," Anna said and rolled her eyes at Mazelle as they went into the kitchen and took seats at the table. "Belle had an interesting day."

"Oh?" Mazelle raised her eyebrows and wondered aloud if they should call Drew up from the barn. Anna and Belle exchanged looks and they both nodded, so Mazelle sent Joey to get his dad and then started putting cookies on a plate and pouring more glasses of milk. In a few minutes Joey returned with Drew.

"What's up?" Drew asked looking around the table.

"I had an interesting first day of school here," Belle said, and she explained what had happened in the school administration office with the secretary, and how she had explained her resemblance to Mazie.

"I didn't know what else to say. I wasn't expecting to be noticed, I guess. And for sure I wasn't expecting to be grilled," Belle finished.

"I'm sorry, Belle. We should have talked about this. It did cross my mind the first time you mentioned that you might want to stay here, but then I forgot. Did it upset you?"

"Not really. I thought the secretary was rude, but maybe she was just shocked and curious and, well, you should have seen her face!" Belle chuckled at the memory. "After I told her that I was adopted and who my dad was, and where we lived, she couldn't get me on my way fast enough. That part was kind of funny. After that, I was ready for the funny looks I got the rest of the day."

"Well," Mazie said with a cheeky grin. "You really can't blame them for looking twice! We are both gorgeous, after all!" The twins groaned, but everyone else laughed and the tension around the table eased a bit.

"I'm glad you told the truth, sweetheart, that's always the best way to handle things." Drew said with a smile. "Liz and I are both proud to claim you as our daughter. The shock factor will wear off fairly quickly, I think."

Mazelle had noticed Joey and Wyatt exchanging meaningful looks.

"Did you boys have something to say?"

"Well isn't the school secretary Mrs. Brown? From our church?" Wyatt asked.

"Yes," Drew said. "Why?"

"Because she shouldn't have been surprised at all," Joey explained. "She already asked us all about Belle at Vacation Bible School."

"She did? What did she want to know?"

"She said she'd seen us with a pretty older girl who looked like Mazie. She asked if she was our cousin or something." Wyatt said. "She said 'or something' in a weird way."

"And we said that she was our sister," Joey added. "And then she said there must have been some funny business while you were in the service."

"And what did you say?" Drew asked quietly, his jaw tight. Wyatt squared his shoulders and looked his dad in the eye.

"I said it wasn't funny. Our mom had to send Belle away to another family so she wouldn't get her life ruined by nasty old gossips, and it made her cry." There was shocked silence around the table. Drew turned to Joey and waited expectantly.

"And I said our dad was wounded fighting for our country, and we were real proud of him." Joey said, looking steadily back at his father.

"You weren't rude?" Drew asked.

"We were polite, Dad. She was the one that was nasty," Wyatt assured him, and Joey nodded.

"Well done, both of you. Did she say anything else, or ask any more questions?" Wyatt and Joey shook their heads. "Why didn't you mention this to us when it happened?"

The boys exchanged a look and then Joey said. "Remember when that coach from another town called me names during the little league game and you told me adults can be bullies?" Drew nodded. "Well, I think Mrs. Brown is a bully. She says mean things, in a way that sounds nice, but it isn't, you know?"

"And she never does it when other adults are around," Wyatt added. "We don't like her."

"Thank you both for sticking up for me and your parents. You are my heroes!" Belle said just as Liz walked into the kitchen. Joey and Wyatt covered their embarrassment by grabbing more cookies on their way out of the kitchen to do their chores.

"Who did something heroic?" Liz wanted to know. So they went through the whole story all over again, and Liz agreed with Drew that Belle had done the right thing in answering questions honestly even though they were rude.

Belle repeated the story one more time for Matt that evening. He said that the truth was nothing to be ashamed of. As for Mrs. Brown's attitude, he just said it takes all kinds.

The hoopla over Belle's appearance died down within a few weeks. She earned a spot on the school newspaper and joined the choir. By Halloween she had a few friends and had settled in at her new school.

"Dad!" Belle said when he got home from work in mid-December. "Grandma Mazelle says James and Pete and their families are coming here for Christmas! And Grandma and Grandpa Baxter. Adam and John aren't coming because they are spending the holiday with their wives' families."

"So there are lots of new cousins to meet!" Matt commented.

"Eleven! I can hardly wait!"

"Do you feel left out with all of them sleeping in the bunkhouse and you sleeping here?"

Belle grinned at him, "Not really. By bedtime, I'm ready for some quiet time."

With Mazie, Wyatt and Joey to break the ice, it took only a few minutes for Belle to be accepted as one of the "greats" as they called themselves. Soon they were chatting away as if they'd always been family.

"Grandma Mazelle says you go to college in Bozeman. Do you like it?" Belle asked Will.

"I like it a lot." Will replied. "I've made a bunch of new friends, and I like being in college. Are you planning to go next year?"

"I'm thinking about living at home and going to Northern," Belle replied. "I don't think I'm ready to move again, yet."

"Drew and Liz wouldn't want you to go so soon, either, since they just found you again."

"Do you think that's weird?" Belle asked cautiously. "That I'm their daughter, but I had an adoptive family, too, I mean?"

"Not really. I don't see what the big deal is. There are a couple of girls in one of my classes who are expecting, and they aren't married. I think they are going to keep their babies." Will shrugged. "I'm just glad our family got you back. I always figured we would, someday."

"What do you mean, you always figured...? You knew about me. Before this year, I mean?" Belle said suspiciously. Will glanced around to make sure they wouldn't be overheard.

"Yeah, well, I wasn't supposed to, but sometimes if kids are quiet enough, parents and grandparents forget they are around. I heard lots of stuff I wasn't supposed to hear." Will winked. "I've known about you since I was pretty little, so I assume all the adults in the family knew fairly early on. When I was about eight or so, I asked Grandma Mazelle why we never saw our cousin Belle." He grinned at the memory.

"What did she say?"

"Well, she doesn't lie – ever – so she told me that Liz couldn't take care of you by herself so you had different parents and lived somewhere else. She told me it was something only the grown-ups talked about, and that I wasn't supposed to tell the rest of the cousins." Will smirked.

"So...did you keep the secret?" Belle wanted to know, but guessed the answer by the look on Will's face.

"I did for awhile, but she forgot to make me promise, and, well, kids have their own code of honor, you know." He paused and looked at her with raised eyebrows. "Or maybe you don't since you grew up as an only child?"

"No siblings and no cousins close to my age, so I don't know anything about this, um, code. Tell me." Belle demanded.

"Basically, when it comes to secrets of any kind, it is us against them." Will explained. "I'm the oldest, and I knew a secret, so when Rachael was twelve and Emily and Marcus were thirteen, I told them, and we had our own little club. Since then as each one of my cousins got to be twelve or so, I, or I should say 'we', let them in on the secret, and they joined the club."

"You rat!" Belle giggled. "I love it!" But then she frowned. "Wait a minute, but Mazie and the twins didn't know."

"Yeah, well that's where it got complicated." Will nodding. "There were six of us who knew. We were going to tell Mazie when she was twelve, but then we didn't because it was her sister we were talking about, and finding out you had an older sister you didn't know about is a lot different than hearing about a lost cousin. So we chickened out and didn't tell her."

"So that was the end of it?" Belle wanted to know.

"You've met my sister Rachael, right?" Will asked with raised eyebrows.

"Yesterday." Belle agreed, grinning. Rachael and Will both had sandy brown hair and hazel eyes, but where Will was mellow, Rachael practically vibrated with energy. Belle could imagine she would be hard to ignore if she wanted something.

"Well, when you know her better you'll understand. She nagged me to death! She kept saying that if she had a lost sister, she would want to know."

"Well? Tell me the rest."

Will rolled his eyes. "As usual, Rach got her way. The twins were almost twelve, so we decided to tell them and Mazie at Christmas. We were trying to figure out if we should have two ceremonies, one for Mazie and the twins and one for the cousins, or tell them all at the same time. Then we had a big blizzard and Mom got sick, so we ended up staying home for Christmas." Will flashed Belle a mischievous grin. But Belle was frowning at him.

"Back up a minute. What kind of ceremonies are you talking about?"

"That kind of information wasn't something we just blurted out, you know." Will exclaimed. "It had to be presented at a secret club meeting after dark, with a blood oath."

"Really? A blood oath?" Belle asked with wide eyes.

"Oh yeah! Nothing awful, I promise," Will assured her.

"A blood oath sounds awful to me," Belle objected.

"Okay! Okay! Don't freak out!" He glanced around again to make sure their conversation was still private. "You know that the kids usually sleep in the bunkhouse at family gatherings." Belle nodded. "So after everyone went to bed, we'd get up and bring whoever was old enough to join our club into the bathroom and light a candle. One of us explained that we had a secret and asked if they wanted to know and would swear not to tell. They always said yes, of course."

"Oh, of course!" Belle agreed, rolling her eyes.

Will grinned and went on. "Then I unrolled the scroll, slowly, to build the suspense, you know, and had each of them read the oath out loud and put their signature and the date underneath the signatures of the older cousins and the dates they had signed. When everyone had done that, we brought out a needle and each one ran it through the candle flame to sterilize it. Then they poked their finger, and put a bloody fingerprint beside their name. After that, we told them what we knew about you."

"I can't believe you did that!"

"It was pretty cool. When the fingerprints were dry, I rolled the scroll back up and sealed it with a drop of wax from the candle." Will finished. "Oh, and we all agreed that if anyone found out anything about you, we would share it with the others."

"So where is this secret scroll?"

"I kept it locked up in my safe box in my closet at home unless we were inducting someone into the group. Now we won't need it, I guess." Belle shook her head, but couldn't keep from grinning.

"Weren't you afraid one of the cousins would let something slip?" She asked.

"We all took the blood oath thing seriously, so I was pretty sure nobody would tell." Will said. Belle cocked her head at him. "Okay, I was a little worried when everything went public last spring and you came to stay with Anna. I didn't know if they could act surprised by the news, but they all did. I don't think the adults ever suspected a thing."

On Christmas Eve the family gathered in the living room to open their gifts before attending midnight church services. Torn wrapping paper and discarded ribbons littered the floor when Belle took a package from the bag she had carried in and quietly handed it to Liz. Everyone else was busy cleaning up or admiring Mazelle's painting of the farmhouse from Anna. Drew had noticed though, and moved quietly to stand behind Liz, resting a supportive hand on her shoulder as she removed the ribbon and paper and opened the box. There lay a pink photo album completely filled with pictures of Belle. On the first page, she was dressed in a green gown and wrapped in a yellow and green print blanket. Tears trickled down Liz's cheeks, and Drew's eyes were bright as he watched Liz leaf through the pages one by one. The last picture was from Belle's seventeenth birthday party.

"Thank you so much, Belle." Liz whispered.

"When we moved our stuff here from Laramie, my dad found this. There were two identical albums, so Mom must always have wanted to give this one to you," Belle said, her voice clogged with unshed tears.

"This was her way of sharing your childhood with me. Bless her heart!" Liz said in wonder as she cradled the album.

"Yeah. And I feel better. Obviously she planned to tell me eventually," Belle said softly.

"What's going on here?" Caro asked in concern, her voice quiet.

"Belle just gave me this photo album, Mom. It has all her baby pictures in it." Liz explained to her mother. "Debbie kept two albums, so I could have one. Look, she even wrote little notes." Caro took the album and turned the pages slowly, and her eyes filled with tears, too. Soon there was a small crowd around the album and someone was handing around a box of tissues. Belle had moved to stand beside her dad.

"I'm glad you found that box, Dad," she said as she gave him a hug.

"Me too, honey." Matt said, returning her hug. "Me, too."

The rest of the year flew by and in no time at all, graduation was looming. Belle and Mazie were baking cookies when the twins came into the kitchen looking for a snack.

"We don't want you to get a big head or anything," Wyatt teased her.

"Yeah, it's our job to keep you humble. That's what brothers do." Joey agreed.

"Humble about what?" Belle asked, smiling at the twins, who had grown so much during the last year that she now had to look up at them.

"Because everybody is coming to see you graduate," Wyatt elaborated.

"Why would I need to be humble about that?" Belle wanted to know. "I'm thrilled that everybody is coming!"

"Well, you might think they're coming because you are special or something," said Joey.

"I'm *not* special?" Belle asked in mock indignation.

"Nope." Wyatt grinned. "They're just coming because you are the only one graduating this year. It's an excuse for a party, that's all, nothing to do with you, really. You shouldn't take it personally or you'll get a big head."

"Well, I think it has everything to do with me and that makes me very special."

"Next year there will be Emily and Marcus, and the year after that Seth, Rachael and Alison." Joey counted them off on his fingers.

"Yup, then David, Paul, Diane and Maggie are together and Daniel is with Joey and me." Wyatt said.

Mazie interrupted. "There are only four of the greats who are special enough to have a year all to themselves. That would be Will, Belle, me," Mazie took a bow, "and Patrick. The rest of you have to share!"

"Nah, hogging a whole year to yourself makes you four spoiled and selfish, definitely not special!" Wyatt and Joey laughed as they each grabbed a couple of cookies from the cooling rack and ambled out of the kitchen. Mazie and Belle shook their heads and went back to scooping cookie dough onto baking sheets.

"Who comes next after the twins and Daniel?" Belle asked.

"Zeke comes next, and he would have a year of his own, too, but they held him back a year, so he's with Ann Marie & Bob, then Bill and Rebecca are next and Patrick is last, by himself, like us." Mazie answered.

"I still can't keep all that straight without a chart!" Belle sighed.

"Years of practice!" Mazie said airily.

When the entire family gathered for Belle's graduation, there was some talk of getting motel rooms, but they managed to cram everyone into the Edward's house, Anna's house and the bunkhouse. There were people sleeping on couches and air mattresses in living rooms, Mazelle's sewing room, and Anna's sunroom and everyone had to wait in line to use a bathroom, but nobody seemed to mind.

Belle enjoyed everything about the graduation festivities and all the family who showed up to celebrate with her, but she also indulged in a few tears because she missed her mom, and was sorry she couldn't be here to share in the celebration. She had a feeling she would always miss her mom at odd times and special moments throughout her life.

XXI
Life Goes On

"Anna, are you tired of us yet?" Matt asked. Belle looked up and waited. They were sitting around Anna's kitchen table on Saturday morning. It was the week after Belle had graduated from high school.

"Tired of you?" Anna smiled. "No. I like having you around. I'd miss you if you left."

"So I guess we don't have to start looking for a place to move?" Matt asked.

"I think the three of us rub along pretty well together. There's no need for you to get your own place when I have plenty of room, unless you are tired of me, that is."

"Not at all. It's a deal, then. We'll stay!" Matt stuck out his hand to shake on it, while Belle gave the two of them a wide grin and saluted their handshake with her coffee mug.

That summer, Matt helped Belle get a job at the hospital as an aide to the nurse's aides. She called herself an aide-gopher. One day she might read to a restless patient, other days she would run errands, water plants, or deliver meals. She helped wherever they needed her and enjoyed the variety of jobs and the people she met and worked with. The job was supposed to be for the summer, but in August her supervisor told her if she wanted to continue working while she went to college, they'd love to have her, and would arrange her schedule around her classes. She said yes to that idea.

The shop teacher at Havre High School retired at the end of the school year and the school board offered Drew his position. Drew was excited about becoming a full-time teacher. He got busy formulating lesson plans and projects and was a little worried about getting everything done at home. Wyatt and Joey were quite indignant when he mentioned he might need to hire help on the farm.

"What are we, chopped liver?" Joey asked indignantly. "Working on the farm is how we keep our muscles in shape and stay tan! Girls love tan guys with muscles."

"I'm pretty sure we can help you out, Dad," Wyatt added, "Course we have years of experience, and you should pay us more for that."

"Yeah, it might be cheaper to hire a total stranger – or Mazie," Joey agreed. The two boys grinned at each other. Mazie rolled her eyes, but otherwise ignored them. She was good at that after years of practice. Drew said he would be happy to pay them top dollar.

"And after I deduct room and board, clothes, shoes and school expenses, if there is anything left, you can save ten percent, give ten percent to charity and spend the rest however you choose."

"Dad!" Joey and Wyatt protested.

"Welcome to the real world."

"You two better just work for free, because I know how many cookies you eat and you really can't afford to pay for your food, much less everything else!" Mazie snickered.

Belle started college knowing she wanted to be a teacher like Liz and Grandma Caro. Soon she was immersed in her classes and before she knew it, three years had flown by, the twins were sophomores earning a reputation for athletic prowess on the basketball court, and Mazie was getting ready to be the lone family member to graduate from high school in the spring.

All the cousins were growing up, too, and it was a challenge to keep track of everybody. She had copied Grandma Mazelle's family letter idea and called it "cousin's correspondence." All the boys had declined to be included, some not very politely.

"Are you nuts?" Marcus had asked incredulously. "Why would I want to write letters at all, and especially to a bunch of girls?"

Will had been a little more subtle. "I'm busy with school. Rach can keep me up to date."

Like the letters that circulated between Grandma Mazelle and her children, Belle and the rest of the girls circulated letters that informed each other of their activities and special events. When the packet of letters arrived, the recipient read everyone else's letter, removed her own old letter and wrote a new one, then sent the packet to the next person on the list. They had agreed not to keep the letter for more than two days, so with ten participants, and allowing for mail time, the letter made the rounds every six weeks or so. Belle was thankful there was a girl in every family except for Bobby and Billy, who belonged to Uncle Adam and Aunt Lynn. Uncle John's daughter Rebecca usually had news of their family, since they lived reasonably close. Although Maggie and her brother Zeke were technically cousins only to the Edwards children and Belle, everyone had agreed that Maggie should be included.

Grandma Mazelle could still rattle off all the details of where everyone was and what they were doing, but Belle kept a list and updated it each time she read the cousin's correspondence, lest she forget something important. Emily and Marcus had graduated two years ago. Marcus was farming with his dad in Townsend, and Emily was living at home and attending classes at Northern Idaho College in Sandpoint, planning to be a teacher like her mother. Rachael, Alison and Seth had graduated the previous spring. Seth had always marched to his own drum, so though his dad was a teacher and his mother was a nurse, he had decided he wanted to be an architect. He was taking classes at Spokane Community College so he could save money by living at home and planned to transfer to a university in another year or so. The girls were following in their mothers' footsteps, Alison in nursing and Rachael in teaching. They were rooming together at MSU in Bozeman. Both of them had been a little nervous about leaving their homes in Colorado and Wyoming, but they were rooming together and with Rachael's brother Will nearby, they were doing fine. Will was in his last year of the engineering program at MSU in Bozeman. He had just gotten engaged to Joanie, who was studying to be a teacher. They were planning a Christmas wedding, after which they planned to return to Bozeman and finish school while living in married student housing.

Grandma Mazelle still walked every day and was mentally sharp as a tack. The family was already planning a big bash during next year's July reunion to celebrate her 90th birthday.

"I'll put it on my calendar, but keep in mind that I'm old. So if I move on to the next life before then, go ahead and have angel food cake anyway," she commented with a smile and a twinkle in her eye.

Anna had finally taken Mazelle's advice and started to display her artwork. Matt and Belle helped her set up a display at the church bazaar in the fall, including placing a modest price on each painting, knowing that Anna would have given them away otherwise.

"Twenty three people bought paintings!" Anna said, totally amazed that they had actually paid for her work. One of the pictures they displayed, although it was not for sale, was the picture she had done of Mazelle's farmhouse, which was now known as the Edwards house. It had generated quite a lot of interest, and several people had asked if she would paint pictures of their homes or other historic buildings of interest to them. She had agreed to do one or two and see how that went before agreeing to do any others. She had begun to sketch the Frank Buttrey home on Second Avenue. It was a colonial style home built in 1919, and since its owner had started the chain of Buttreys grocery stores in 1896, it was of historical significance. She had been asked to paint The First Presbyterian Church on Fourth Avenue, too. Construction of the church was interrupted by World War I and finished after the war. Anna thought painting the stained glass windows would be a challenge, so she was thinking about doing that next.

Belle was immersed in lesson plans and classroom activities for student teaching, and also thinking about her upcoming graduation and finding a teaching position. She hoped to remain in the area if possible. She still didn't want to be very far away from either one of her families. Several of her classmates were engaged, but wedding bells were the furthest thing from Belle's mind.

XXII

Dr. Sam

"Dr. Jackson?" Matt looked up to see a tall good-looking young man in the doorway of his office. He wore a white coat and had a stethoscope sticking out of his pocket.

"Come in, it's Sam, isn't it? Dr. Sam Martinson?"

"You have a good memory, sir. Last time you saw me was during my internship here a year ago." Sam said as he walked in, leaned across the desk to shake hands and then took a seat in one of the chairs Matt motioned to in front of the desk. He was tall and slim with broad shoulders, blond hair and blue eyes.

"I suppose I could simply accept the compliment on my memory," Matt chuckled, "but the truth is I talked to Dr. Jenkins when he was checking your references. I saw him again yesterday and he mentioned you were coming to work at the clinic. If not for that, I'd be scratching my head and saying that you look familiar but I can't figure out why." Sam laughed. Matt added, "I hope you like it over there, they've got a good team."

"I noticed that when I was here. That's one of the reasons I applied for the job." Sam said with a smile. "How was India this time?"

"Everything went well. It was our fifth year and I have to believe we are making a difference with the time we spend there every summer," Matt replied. "Don't get me started, though. I could talk about the India project all day, or maybe even all week. We can save that for another time."

"I look forward to it." Sam said.

"Now, what can I do for you?" Matt asked.

"Well, sir, it's a personal matter."

"Lay it out and I'll see if I can help," Matt encouraged.

"Do you believe in love at first sight, sir?" Matt blinked in surprise.

"Why would you ask me a question like that?"

"Because I don't, or at least I didn't." Sam shook his head. "But then I met a girl during my internship here last year, and my first thought was that she was the one for me. I thought the long hours were making me crazy or something." Sam paused. "I decided I would forget her when I didn't see her almost every day, but I haven't been able to get her out of my mind."

Matt found this very interesting, having had a similar experience when he'd met his own wife. He decided not to share that little fact, however.

"You applied for a job here because of this girl?"

"She's actually the main reason I decided to come back here," Sam said, not looking exactly happy about admitting that. "I can't stop thinking about her."

"Does she feel the same way about you?" Matt asked curiously.

"I don't know, sir," Sam replied, looking embarrassed. "You know how hectic it is being an intern. There isn't really much time to date and since I wasn't planning to be here very long, it didn't seem like a good idea to get involved."

"Are you saying that you think you love a girl you haven't even been on a date with?" Sam nodded. "Well, have you asked her out since you've been back?"

"No, sir. That's the problem. I can't find her."

"You can't find her?"

"She apparently doesn't work here anymore."

"I'm sorry to hear that, especially if one of the reasons you came to work here was to get to know her better. But I don't see how I can help you."

"I don't either, sir, but when I asked the head nurse about her... you know, if she knew where she went, she said to ask you." Sam looked bewildered. "And she looked like she was trying not to laugh."

"That's odd." Matt thought about that for a moment, shrugged and asked. "Well, what's this girl's name?"

"Belle." Matt seemed startled and sat up straight in his chair. "You do know her! Good! All I need is her last name, sir."

"Belle's last name...is Jackson."

Sam gaped at him. When he finally recovered the power of speech, he repeated, "Jackson? Belle is your daughter?" Matt nodded. "But I saw her with..." Sam shook his head, closed his eyes for a moment and took a deep breath. He opened his eyes, looked directly at Matt and began again.

"Sir, I knew you had a daughter studying to be a teacher. I thought you only had one child, and that you were a widower. But since Belle worked here, I thought she was studying nursing." Sam hesitated, clearly confused, but Matt didn't comment so he plowed on. "Then I saw her with a younger girl who looks like her sister. They were with a woman who looks just like them. I assumed that was their mom."

"All of that is true except for the nursing part. Belle has been working here while she went to college, studying to be a teacher. Right now, she's not working here because she is doing her student teaching."

"Okay. So she's your daughter, and you are a widower, but she has a different mom and sister?" Sam asked, frowning.

"It's a long story. But I think it is up to Belle to decide if she wants to share it with you."

"And your number is in the phone book?" Sam asked.

"Our number is in the phone book, yes," Matt agreed.

"Thanks!" Sam said, as he got up to leave. He turned at the door. "Just so you know, sir, I intend to marry her."

"Belle makes her own decisions, Sam. She always has," Matt said. That evening he told Anna all about the strange encounter he'd had with Dr. Sam Martinson.

"So this young, good looking Dr. Sam intends to marry Belle?" Anna asked, her eyes twinkling.

"That's what he said. Should I be concerned?"

"Belle can take care of herself, Matt. She's had dates before." Anna smiled. "This might be interesting, though."

"Why do you say that?" Matt asked.

Anna smiled and shook her head as her mind went back to a sunny afternoon the previous fall. Mazelle and Liz had stopped by and the three of them were sitting outside on the porch sipping iced tea having a nice visit. When Belle got home from work, she poured herself a glass of iced tea and joined them. She related a couple of funny stories about things that had happened at work, and then told them all about the tall, blond, blue-eyed intern who had just started at the hospital that day. "Honestly, the man is so good looking that all the women at the hospital practically swoon when he enters the room," Belle had said with a shake of her head.

Anna remembered too, that Belle had mentioned this young man again several times over the next few months. She said he made her nervous, so she avoided him when she could. And she said that, according to the gossip at the hospital, he didn't date. Oh yes, Anna thought, this was going to be interesting.

Belle was quite shocked to hear from Sam that evening when he called and asked her out. She discovered that they had a lot of things in common. Sam was easy to talk to and as serious about medicine as she was about teaching. It took Sam three dates to get up the courage to ask her about her complicated family history. He was fascinated with her explanation, and he hit it off with the entire Edwards family the first time he met them. It took him six months to gather the courage to ask Belle to marry him, but he needn't have worried. She said yes right away.

Sam stared at the phone on the kitchen counter of his apartment. He didn't quite understand how he could be so happy that Belle had agreed to marry him, and at the same time, so nervous about calling to let his parents know. His mind went back to the conversation he'd had with his two brothers when he was at home for Christmas.

"This girl you're seeing, is it serious?" Ben asked curiously.

"It was serious before she ever agreed to go out with me. I knew I wanted to marry her almost from the first time I saw her. It felt like I'd been struck by lightning." Sam said, grinning and shaking his head at the memory. "At first I thought I was getting a migraine or something." Ben looked at him in surprise and Tim snickered.

"Lightning? Are you kidding me? Geez, Sam, you're a doctor! I thought you had a scientific mind and all that. You sound like a romantic!" Tim scoffed.

"I know. It is embarrassing to talk about, but that's what it felt like. I couldn't get her out of my mind, and she didn't seem to notice me at all. I decided to try to forget her while I finished my residency. It didn't work, so I applied for a job at the clinic in Havre."

"He's a goner all right," Ben said to Tim, who nodded in agreement, shaking his head.

"You don't even know the whole story!" Sam said, with a laugh. Then he told them about the embarrassing conversation he'd had with Belle's dad, and both of them roared with laughter.

"Belle is totally perfect for me. I got a ring and everything. I'm just waiting for the right time to ask her, and doing everything I can to make sure that when I do, she says 'yes'."

"Do Mom and Dad know?" Tim asked.

"Well, they know I'm seeing her, but I haven't said I'm serious. No point in that until she says yes, is there?" Sam asked. Tim and Ben exchanged looks and didn't reply. "Okay, what's going on?" Sam asked looking from one brother to the other.

"Twice for me," Ben said, looking at Tim.

"Same here." Tim agreed.

"What are you guys talking about?"

"Girls, or I guess I should say, *women* since we are not kids anymore." Ben said.

"What about women?"

"I took one home when I was in law school. Something about getting near the end of school, and you start to think about settling down, I guess. Anyway, I'd been dating Linda for a few months so one weekend I took her home with me. I don't know if I was serious about her or not. I hadn't been thinking about buying a ring, but after that weekend, we broke up."

"Why?" Sam asked.

"Mom didn't like her," Ben replied.

"How do you know that?"

"Oh, come on, Sam, we can all tell when Mom isn't happy about something, you know that." Tim said, with an irritated look.

"Same thing happened to me my senior year. Her name was Ellen. I wasn't ready to buy a ring either, but we had fun together and I liked her, so I took her home one weekend, and Mom didn't like her, so," he shrugged, "that was that."

"Did you ask Mom about it?" Sam asked, starting to get nervous.

"Not me," Ben said, "Did you?" he asked his brother. Tim shook his head.

"So you don't know what it was that she didn't like?" Both brothers shook their heads.

"It happened again last year, though," Ben said. "Her name was Jill. She's an attorney with another law firm. I met her at a political fundraiser and we hit it off. We'd been dating for several months, so I took her home one weekend, and there was disapproval all over the place."

"Me, too," Tim said. "Last month with Pam. She's a flight attendant, smart, pretty and fun to be with. But for some reason, Mom didn't like her."

"What about Dad?" Sam asked, beginning to panic.

"Dad likes everyone, especially people who like his kids," Ben said, and Tim nodded.

That was when Sam had decided that he wasn't going to introduce Belle to his family until she had agreed to marry him. Now she had said yes and he needed to let his mother know. Best to get it done, he thought, as he picked up the phone.

XXIII

Full Disclosure

"Hi, Mom," Sam said. "I have some great news!" He hoped she couldn't hear the fake cheerfulness in his voice.

"Oh, honey, tell me!"

"I'm getting married!"

"Married? We didn't even know you were serious about a girl! When did this happen?"

"She said yes tonight."

"Tell me about her," Andrea demanded. So Sam told his mother about Belle and her job at the hospital, how he'd met her during his internship and tried to forget her, but couldn't, and how after six months, he had finally had the courage to ask her and she had agreed to marry him.

"She's the best thing that ever happened to me," he said earnestly, hoping against hope that she and his dad would not have any objections to Belle. He knew he was going to marry her, regardless, but he loved his parents and wanted their approval.

"Of course you asked her father for permission to propose, right?" Andrea asked. Sam was silent. "Sam! You didn't ask her father?"

"I didn't know I had to do that."

"You should, Sam! It's the proper thing to do," Andrea insisted.

"Okay, I'll talk to him tomorrow," Sam said.

"And when you talk to him, you can invite him and his wife and Belle here for Easter so we can get to know them," Andrea decreed.

"He's a widower, so it's just him and Belle."

"That's fine, Sam, invite Belle and her dad. Okay?" Sam could tell that Andrea wasn't going to take no for an answer.

"Yeah, okay, I'll ask them," Sam agreed, somewhat reluctantly, and said good-bye.

Dr. Paul Martinson walked into the kitchen from the garage just as his wife hung up the phone. He smiled at her, "Talking to one of the boys?"

Andrea nodded. "Sam is engaged."

"Wonderful!" Paul exclaimed with a big grin. "When is the wedding? I was beginning to wonder if any of our boys were going to find the right girl."

"They haven't set a date yet, at least he didn't mention one. I told him to invite the girl, her name is Belle, and her dad here for Easter so we can meet them"

"Good idea. What about her mother? Are her parents divorced?"

"No, Sam said her dad was a widower."

"That had to be tough," Paul said as he poured himself a glass of ice water and pulled a stool up to the island. "Tell me all about this girl."

Andrea shared the few details Sam had given her. "I don't know very much, really. He didn't seem to want to talk, and I got the feeling he wasn't too crazy about bringing her here for Easter, either."

"That's not like him. Do you think the girl is pregnant and that's why he is marrying her?"

Andrea shrugged. "Don't know. I suppose we'll find out." She contemplated her own nearly empty glass of ice water and asked curiously, "Did you like either of the girls Ben brought home?"

"I liked them both, and I liked the girls Tim brought home, too," Paul replied. "I guess the boys didn't like them enough." Paul shook his head and added. "I really want them to find good women. I'd like some grandchildren before I'm too old and decrepit to play with them."

"We did start later than a lot of people, didn't we?" Andrea teased. She and Paul had agreed that it was better to have their education finished before starting a family. Then it had taken longer than they thought for the first baby to come along, so Andrea had started her career, too. Ben had been born when she was thirty five, followed by Tim two years later and Sam just before her fortieth birthday.

"We did," Paul agreed with a smile, "My first priority for the boys is for them to have good marriages. Like you and me. Then, I want grandchildren!" He winked at her, put his empty glass in the dishwasher and asked if she planned to swim tonight. They usually did laps in the pool after work and then cooked their evening meal together.

"I'll be out in a few minutes, dear." She joined him a few minutes later and as she swam, she pondered Sam and his engagement. Andrea agreed that the girls Ben and Tim had brought here to meet them had been pretty and friendly, and they had jobs they seemed to enjoy. The trouble was, that, as a psychologist, she spent her days counseling people who built their lives on relationships that were not very strong or particularly deep. She wanted her sons to have the kind of relationship that she and Paul had, where the strength of their bond with each other was the basis for every-thing else they did. She knew that mothers tend to be very critical of the women their sons date and she wondered if that's what she was doing. She shook her head as she got out of the pool and picked up a towel to dry off. No, she decided, that wasn't it. She believed with all her heart that the marital relationship was the foundation for the family. As usual, she and Paul were in agreement on the important things; she wanted grandchildren too, but first she wanted all of her sons to find women they could build lives and grow old with.

Her thoughts turned to Sam. Once he set his mind on something, he pursued it with single-minded purpose. He'd been that way since he was a small boy. It sound-ed like he had chosen the woman he wanted to be his wife, and Andrea knew there would be no changing his mind. She hoped he had chosen wisely, and was glad that she would know one way of the other in about ten days.

Sam knocked on Matt's office door, which was ajar. "Dr. Jackson?" Matt looked up from his desk. "Could I talk to you for a minute?"

"Yeah, come on in. What is it?"

"Well, sir, I talked to my mother last night," Sam said, grimly, standing stiffly in front of Matt's desk instead of taking a seat.

"Is that bad?" Matt asked worriedly. "Nothing wrong at home, I hope."

"No, everyone is fine. Thing is, I called to tell my parents that Belle agreed to marry me."

"And she wasn't happy about that?" Matt asked, frowning.

"I think it would be more accurate to say she wasn't happy with me, because I didn't come and ask you for permission first."

"Oh," Matt said.

"She said I needed to make sure we have your blessing."

"You do, Sam. Belle thinks the two of you were made for each other. And if she's happy, I'm happy."

"Thank you, sir, and there's something else."

"Yeah?"

"My mom wants you and Belle to come for Easter to meet them."

Matt looked at him carefully. "Do *you* want us to come and meet your family?"

"I would love to have you both meet my family."

"I don't know one thing about your family. I hope Belle knows at least the basics." Matt raised his eyebrows at Sam, who sighed.

"She knows the basics. My dad, Paul, is a surgeon and my mom, Andrea, is a psychologist. They are both very good at what they do. My oldest brother Ben is a lawyer and Tim is a commercial airline pilot. I'm the youngest." Sam didn't seem inclined to elaborate.

"I can probably get away for a few days, but it would help to know where we are going."

"Oh, sorry. Texas. Castle Hills. It's about twenty miles from San Antonio."

"So we'd fly into San Antonio, then?" Sam nodded. "I think I can clear my schedule for a few days, if Belle can."

"I'll talk to her tonight." Sam said, but he didn't sound happy about it.

Later that night, he broached the subject to Belle. They were on Anna's porch watching the sunset. Sam had been pre-occupied during supper and Belle was about to ask him if something was wrong when he spoke. "I talked to my mom last night and she wants me to invite you and your dad for Easter to meet them."

"That sounds fun," Belle said. "I'll check with Dad, but I know I can go." Sam told her that he'd talked to Matt that afternoon and he said he could clear his schedule for the trip.

"You don't seem thrilled about it. Are you afraid your family won't like me?"

Sam didn't answer for so long that Belle wondered if he was going to respond. Finally, he explained.

"Ben and Tim have both taken girls home to meet Mom and Dad, and then they broke up. They said Mom didn't approve of the girls."

"So you are afraid your parents, or at least your mom, won't like me."

"I don't see how anyone could not like you. But I don't know what she didn't like about those girls. Maybe nobody will be good enough for any of her sons."

"You worry too much." Belle tried to soothe him, but she had more than a few doubts herself, and ten days later, seated in Dr. Andrea Martinson's living room, she had to work at staying relaxed.

Andrea Martinson was a beautiful woman, a little taller than Belle, with dark blonde hair and crinkly laugh lines around blue eyes that were just like Sam's. She seemed tense, though, and she had seemed tense since Belle and her father had arrived the previous evening. This morning after breakfast, Sam had taken Matt to tour the hospital and join his dad for lunch. He had looked a little worried and seemed reluctant to leave Belle, but Andrea assured him they would have a nice chat and get to know each other. Belle had smiled her agreement, even though she felt like she was about to go on trial.

"You have a beautiful home, Dr. Martinson," she began politely, but before she could go on, Andrea interrupted.

"Oh, you must call me Andrea. There are three doctors in this family now, and all of us prefer our own first names."

"All right, Andrea, then." Belle smiled as she continued to look around appreciatively. "I've never been in an adobe house before. It's elegant and comfortable at the same time."

The rooms were spacious, with arched doorways and large windows that provided a view from every room.

"Thank you. We bought this place when the children were small, and we all love it."

"Did you do the decorating yourself?" Belle asked curiously.

"Yes, I like the southwestern style. It suits the house. Are you interested in decorating?"

"I don't know," Belle said thoughtfully. "I know when a room makes me feel comfortable, but I don't know if I could create that kind of space. I've never tried. I suppose I'll find out when Sam and I have our own place."

"Are you planning to live in Havre?"

"Yes. If I don't get a teaching job there, I'll substitute for awhile." Belle went on to explain that they'd been looking for a house to rent and that they planned to use some of the furniture she and her dad had stored when they moved in with Anna. When that subject was exhausted, Andrea asked if they were comfortable in the pool house.

"Oh, yes." Belle replied. "Drew and Liz have a space we call a bunkhouse where guests stay, but that's just sleeping space and a bathroom in the barn. Your pool house has a kitchen and everything. It's beautiful!"

Andrea didn't know how to phrase the questions she had about people sleeping in barns, or who Drew and Liz were, so she changed the subject. "Ben and Tim are coming tomorrow. They're eager to meet you. It'll be the first time we've had everyone here since Christmas."

"I'm looking forward to meeting them, too. I've heard a lot about them, and I love family get-togethers."

"So do I," Andrea agreed. Then, she decided to broach the topic she was most interested in hearing about. "What kind of wedding are you planning, Belle?"

"Sam and I want a small wedding with just family and a few close friends." Belle replied, relieved Andrea had raised a subject she was more than happy to discuss. She was totally in love with Sam and enjoying not only the wedding details, but the prospect of building a life together.

"Really?" Andrea looked surprised. "You don't want a big wedding?"

"Oh, no," Belle laughed. "Sam and I both want it to be meaningful."

"What does that mean, exactly?"

"Well, I'm planning to wear the wedding dress my Great Grandma Mazelle made and the veil that my Great Grandma Amanda made."

"Your great grandmothers are still alive?" Andrea asked.

"Grandma Amanda died when I was small, but Grandma Mazelle will be celebrating her 90th birthday in July."

"Oh. The dress and veil were made for someone else then?"

"Yes, they were made for Grandma Caro, and then Liz wore them, too, so I'll be the third one." Andrea nodded, still looking a little confused. She asked if they had set a date. "Most of the family gets together for a reunion over the 4th of July. I haven't had a chance to talk to Grandma Mazelle yet, but if she doesn't mind, we'd like to get married that weekend, instead of asking everyone to come back another time."

"Do you think she would mind?" Andrea asked.

"Oh no, but the party for her 90th birthday is the 5th and it's only polite to ask, I think."

"Of course," Andrea agreed. "Go on."

"Let's see, oh! I want to have the flowers from Aunt Anna's garden. She grows the most amazing flowers! For pictures, Sam and I have agreed we want a few formal wedding pictures with a professional photographer, but two of my uncles are amateur photographers, so I'm hoping they will do some candid shots of the rehearsal and the wedding party and the reception."

"That sounds very nice."

"The ceremony will be in the church the whole family has been going to for years, and there will be cake after, but then we'll probably have some kind of gathering and a family supper at either Aunt Anna's house or Liz and Drew's place, next door."

"Who are Liz and Drew?" Andrea asked. There was a long pause.

"Sam didn't tell you much about me, did he?" Belle said gently.

"He told us you were the best thing that ever happened to him. But as to the particular details of your life, no, he didn't. Actually, the night he called to tell us he was engaged was the first time he'd talked about you in any detail at all."

"I'm sorry," Belle said. "He really should have warned you. Let me explain." Belle told Sam's mother all about her life as an only child before her mother died, how she'd found out about her adoption and the role her dad's aunt had played in everything. She explained how she came to know her biological family, and that she now considered them to be her family, too.

"I call them my crazy quilt family," she finished, grinning.

"Are they crazy, then?" Andrea asked curiously. Belle laughed.

"Sometimes, I guess they are. Do you know what a crazy quilt is?"

"Not really. I know what a quilt is, of course."

"A crazy quilt is made of scraps of material in random sizes and shapes, in lots of different colors and textures, all stitched together. There isn't any pattern and nothing matches, but the quilt is interesting and unique and keeps you warm."

"I see."

"I think of my family like that, because we have lots of variety and lots of love, and because we're really two families kind of patched together into one."

They chatted for a few minutes about families in general, and Andrea finally asked the question she really wanted the answer for. "How do you feel about being a doctor's wife?"

"The same way I feel about being a doctor's daughter, I guess," Belle answered after a moment of consideration. Andrea raised her eyebrows and waited. Belle stared out the window for a minute and then elaborated. "Well, my dad's a doctor, but he's always been just my dad to me. So I guess what I mean is that I'm in love with Sam because he's Sam. His job wouldn't change how I feel about him."

As Belle explained, the tension seemed to drain away from Andrea and by the time she finished speaking, Andrea was smiling happily.

"You are perfect for Sam, you really are!"

"I'm glad you think so," Belle blushed.

"Let me explain why I've been giving you the third degree. In the last five or six years, Ben and Tim have each brought two girls home to meet us. Thankfully they haven't proposed to any of them."

"Was something wrong with them?"

"Oh, they were nice enough, and they were certainly pretty, but all of them were looking for successful husbands, and it seemed to me that they were more interested in the career than in the man, if you know what I mean." Andrea paused and then added, "Not one of them would want home-grown flowers or be excited about wearing a family wedding dress, much less sharing their wedding weekend with someone's else birthday party, I'm sure of that."

Belle chuckled. "Is that what you were expecting from me?"

Andrea looked embarrassed. "I guess I thought that you might be someone more interested in being a doctor's wife than in being married to Sam. I can see that isn't the case, and I can't tell you how happy I am about that!"

"If I had been, what would you have done?" Belle asked curiously.

"I would have tried to make the best of it, dear, because Sam has already made his choice. There isn't anything else a mother can do in a situation like that. If I voiced any objections and I turned out to be right, nobody would be grateful. And if I voiced any objections and I turned out to be wrong, nobody would ever forget."

"Yes, I see what you mean," Belle said thoughtfully. Then she laughed. "I can't wait for you to meet Grandma Mazelle and Liz, and Aunt Anna, and my two grandmas, Caro and Jean. You will fit right in!"

That's how Sam found them, laughing and chatting as if they'd known each other for years. He relaxed for the first time since he'd told his mother he was engaged. Everything was going to be all right.

XXIV

Wedding Bells

Belle sat on the porch with Mazelle and Liz, all of them enjoying glasses of lemonade on a warm day at the end of April. Belle had just finished telling them about meeting Sam's mother and the conversation they'd had.

"I think I like Andrea Martinson already," Mazelle laughed. "It sounds to me like her sons take her advice, even when she doesn't say a word."

"I wonder if she could give us lessons on how to do that," Liz teased. All three women chuckled.

"Now please tell us about Sam's dad," Mazelle requested, sipping on her lemonade.

"Dr. Paul Martinson. Well, looking at him I can see what Sam will look like when he's older. He's tall and good looking and he has kind eyes. They are a different shade of blue than Sam's. Sam has his mom's eyes. Anyway, Paul and Andrea seem like they communicate without words half the time. My mom and dad did that. And they look at each other the same way Liz and Drew do." She smiled at Liz and continued, "And he is so proud of his sons and their accomplishments. He told me he really wants grand-children, and I think he'll be a good grandfather." Mazelle nodded in satisfaction. The Martinsons sounded like her kind of people.

"Are you and Sam planning to have children any time soon?" Liz asked eagerly.

"Graduation first, then the wedding, then we'll see about kids." She turned to Mazelle. "Grandma, Sam and I are trying to find a good time to have the wedding, and I was wondering what you think about having it on the Saturday after the 4th of July?"

"That's a wonderful idea, dear. We'll already have lots of family here for the re-union." Liz nodded too, murmuring her agreement.

"That's why I thought of that date, but we are also celebrating your birthday. We don't want to horn in on your party," Belle said.

"Belle, dear, I would love to share my party with you and Sam. You should ask yourself if the two of you want to share your wedding with an old lady!"

"No problem!" Belle assured her. And so the wedding date was set for six weeks after Belle was scheduled to graduate with her teaching degree, during the same week most of the family planned to gather for their annual reunion and to celebrate Mazelle's 90th birthday.

Mazelle smiled as Joey and Wyatt escorted her to her seat near the front of the church. As she waited for the wedding to start, she thought back to the previous evening. At the rehearsal dinner, Matt had shared the story of how Sam had asked him for Belle's last name so he could call and ask her for a date, not realizing Matt was her dad. They all had a good laugh, especially when Matt repeated that Sam had said he intended to marry Belle, because he knew when he met her that she was the one for him.

The mood turned more serious after dinner when Matt presented Belle with a small box. She opened it to find a beautiful ring set with a diamond between a purple stone and a green one.

"It's a unique ring because we are a unique family." Matt explained. "Drew and Liz and I hope this ring always reminds you of how much you are loved, by all of your parents." He cleared his throat and continued. "Your mom's birthday was in April, so this diamond from her wedding ring is also her birthstone. Diamonds signify love, and your mom loved you very much." He kissed her cheek and returned to his seat. Drew rose from his seat to speak next.

"The peridot is one of only a few gemstones that exist in just one color, green. It is the birthstone for August, the month Liz was born. Ancient Egyptians called it the gem of the sun because they believed it glowed with an inner light. May you always glow with an inner light, Belle, just as Liz does." He sat down, and Liz stood up to finish the presentation.

"Your birthstone is the amethyst, which comes in varying shades of purple. The ancient Greeks believed the amethyst imparted sincerity and peace of mind. You already possess sincerity and we wish you peace of mind, now and always." Liz smiled at Belle as she sank back into her seat.

Belle was so overcome with emotion that she couldn't speak, but her radiant smile and brimming eyes made words unnecessary. She slipped the ring onto the fourth finger of her right hand and held it up for everyone to see.

Belle was as beautiful a bride as Caro and Liz had been on their wedding days, wearing the same dress and veil. Mazie was her maid of honor, Joey and Wyatt were ushers. The rest of the family, including grandparents, aunts, uncles, and cousins, packed the church.

Belle walked down the aisle on her Matt's arm, stopping in front of the altar where Sam waited with a smile on his face and love in his eyes. When the pastor asked who gave this woman to this man, Liz and Drew stood and together with Matt, the three of them said, "We do."

Belle was not so naïve as to think that she and Sam would sail through life with no problems, but as they repeated their traditional wedding vows to each other, she was sure they would get through whatever life held in store. Their crazy quilt family, which now included Sam's parents and his two brothers, would be there to support and encourage them during tough times and help them celebrate the good ones.

Vivian McDermott is a native Montanan who graduated high school in Conrad and earned her degree at Montana State University. She and her husband still reside in the town of Shelby, where they raised their family together.

www.ingramcontent.com/pod-product-compliance
Lightning Source LLC
Chambersburg PA
CBHW071245130626
46556CB00003B/1171